THIS WAS MY POTTSVILLE

THIS WAS MY POTTSVILLE

Life and Crimes During the Gilded Age

*Breweries * Ballots * Bedlam * Bullets *Barons*

J. Robert Zane

iUniverse, Inc.

New York Lincoln Shanghai

This was my Pottsville
Life and Crimes During the Gilded Age

iUniverse books may be ordered through booksellers or by contacting:

iUniverse
2021 Pine Lake Road, Suite 100
Lincoln, NE 68512
www.iuniverse.com
1-800-Authors (1-800-288-4677)

ISBN-13: 978-0-595-36559-3 (pbk)
ISBN-13: 978-0-595-80990-5 (ebk)
ISBN-10: 0-595-36559-0 (pbk)
ISBN-10: 0-595-80990-1 (ebk)

Printed in the United States of America

"I am a part of all that I have met."

—Lord Alfred Tennyson

Introduction

Pottsville, Pennsylvania, a small city located in that northeast section of the Keystone state commonly referred to as the "anthracite coal region," was founded in 1806 by the industrious John Pott, who had purchased a furnace in anticipation of prosperity in the burgeoning iron industry. He quickly constructed an iron plant as the anthracite coal would be a plentiful and inexpensive fuel to cast molten metal from the furnaces. Soon workmen arrived and set up homes near the Pott furnace. Pottsville was starting its ascent to economic prosperity.

In 1906, the city held a legendary centennial celebration commemorating one hundred years of development; and the townspeople were all firmly convinced that the best was yet to come.

Now, in 2006, during Pottsville's bicentennial period, readers will glimpse back at the town as it was during the gilded age, when men and women predicted Pottsville's eventual economic triumph and its ability to be a contender with the cities of Philadelphia and Pittsburgh. Pottsville's ascent would continue after the centennial, but its ascent would be short-lived; its peak was reached during World War I and its population has been in decline for decades.

Yes, something went wrong along the way, but for a time Pottsville believed it could have been a major contender.

Relive the era from 1906 to 1917, a time of peace and prosperity as recalled by a gentleman by the name of Augustus B. Traut, a Pottsville native, who was in the midst of many of the early events in the city's history, and fortunately was able to give his oral history prior to the 1956 sesquicentennial which coincidently was the year of his death. Traut had given interviews in which he recalled the glorious party held in 1906 and the area's most colorful characters, from the politicians, businessmen, and brewers to the low-life murderers and thugs.

This story was painstakingly recreated from hours of interviews as well as Traut's private notes and placed into book form. The opening italicized paragraphs of each chapter are the words spoken by Auggie Traut during his interviews. These personal remarks will hopefully give the reader a more continuous flow to the story of the early days of Pottsville as well as revealing the unique personality of Auggie Traut, "the living camera" of Pottsville, as he recounts the early twentieth century in his city. Mr. Traut, in his later years was considered one of Pottsville's street people, and his ragged, gruff exterior hid the mind of a great historian and fact-keeper.

PART I

▼

CHAPTER 1

▼

A TIME TO CELEBRATE

It was grandest of times; I can vouch for it, as I was there in those early years employed as a young cub reporter for the Miners Journal Newspaper. Getting the newspaper job meant so much to me as I wanted to make my family so proud. I wouldn't have to work in the mines or the rolling mills as my father and uncles had. Boy! My first real job in my native Pottsville, the rising star in the state, was icing on the cake. You are interested in hearing about the centennial, so that is where I will start. I remember 1906 as if it was only yesterday.

My parents were some of the earliest settlers. From stories that were told to me, when the 19th century dawned upon the wilderness which covered the treasures of coal hidden in the hills of Schuylkill County, there was only one single dwelling built by a pioneer family within the area now referred to as Pottsville. This simple, lonely log house stood down in the valley where the mill on Mauch Chunk Street was later constructed. If I had a map, then I would show you. About the time of the Revolutionary War, Indians murdered the white settlers, supposedly on a Sunday morning when the family rested from normal chores. Two children were murdered there with the parents. I think the last name was Nieman.

My family did not go back that far, that's for sure. I never heard of a family member having trouble with Indians. You say that you are working on a history of the city and were told that I know a lot about this place? Well, you are correct. I remember the good, the bad and the indifferent. I am a walking encyclopedia on the city's history even though I don't look like one. People say that anyone who has my appearance probably knows nothing. They are wrong.

As I mentioned, I'll start with the good times that I remember. I am referring to Old Home Week. Let me tell you about that special time, day by day. Damn, they were good times here in the coal region. I also know a lot about the city's dark side, it's underbelly. I can tell you about a most bizarre murder that occurred when I was a young man. Yes indeed, bizarre it was. I covered that story too. That happened several years later after the centennial. You will just have to wait. That murder is a part of the town's lost history and I will recount it for you, as long as I get to tell you about everything else about the city. Everything and maybe even some more than you would like to know. I don't get many visitors anymore. I am glad you called on me. Let me begin with my story.

No time to think about anything sorrowful or worrisome. It was a time to celebrate!

On weekends Pottsville, a town nestled within seven hills, was one of the preferred Schuylkill county towns to visit, whether you were an anthracite coal miner or a highly educated professional. From all indications, the town and county seat, located in the southern anthracite coalfield of Pennsylvania, was beloved by all ethnic groups and economic classes. It certainly had competition, as another popular county town to visit was Shenandoah located in the middle anthracite coalfield, fifteen miles to the north of Pottsville.

On most Saturdays Pottsville swelled with its visitors, including the miners who spent their precious free time and precious meager earnings on all that the town had to offer. Coal mining was hard, dangerous work. In the late 19th century some observers estimated that three miners were killed every other day in the anthracite fields. When the weekend arrived, mere survival was a good enough reason for a miner to celebrate. The town of Pottsville offered saloons, gambling, restaurants, theatres, dance halls and the many stores that lined Centre Street, the business district located in the heart of the town. While Pottsville offered more than forty-four saloons, hundreds more were found in other parts of the county. So the saloons were not the main attraction by any means. Alcohol was plentiful in Schuylkill County, which had a population of approximately 200,000 and an estimated 1100 saloons serving refreshments to its drinking men (most saloons being off-limits to the ladies). By comparison, Philadelphia, the largest city in the state, had 1700 saloons for a population of two million. Many complain that the saloon licenses in the coal region were given out too freely, and the quality of life was being hurt.

However, that was the way it was back then, in 1906, the centennial year.

The Pennsylvania Centre Turnpike was not the first large-scale road system in the state, as turnpikes dated back as far as the 1700's. The Centre Turnpike was chartered in 1805, connecting Reading to the southeast with Sunbury seventy-five miles to the northwest. In between those two communities the roadway went through an area, later known as Pottsville, and Centre Street, was Pottsville's main thoroughfare.

As acknowledged, the weekends generally attracted throngs of people but in September 1906, the centennial year, the crowds increased beyond anyone's imagination. Pottsville, the small town mid-way on the old Centre Turnpike, was celebrating its one hundredth anniversary with weeklong festivities occurring the first week of September. At the same time young George Simon, Jr. was beginning his middle year at the public high school.

"Did you hear about the episode involving the young Simon boy?"

That curious remark would be echoed throughout Pottsville in just three short years.

CHAPTER 2

▼

SUNDAY

My father came to Pottsville from the Reading area just before the Civil War. He first stayed at White Horse Hotel, which had been constructed in 1818, on the present site of the Necho Allen Hotel. He was not an educated man, and sought out employment at the Rolling Mills in the Fishbach section of the town. He worked there as well as for the Sparks & Parker Foundry, located on East Norwegian Street. He also did some coal mining later in Yorkville; he certainly was not a lazy man.

Now I will tell you about the events that occurred during Old Home Week on Sunday. Are you a religious man? I used to be. I had been married in St. John the Baptist German Catholic Church. My wife was a German girl from Yorkville. Father Frederick Longinus performed the ceremony. They don't make priests like that anymore. My wife and I attended Mass every Sunday and every Holy Day of Obligation, but after my wife filed for divorce, I drifted to a few of the other local churches. For a time I spent a lot of time at the Christian Science Church on West Market Street. Lately I go to the Salvation Army, but I have no allegiance to anyone or anything.

I like to read a lot, as you can see from my extensive library. From my appearance you may think I am not well read, but don't be deceived. Look at my mind and hear me out. Let me continue with the events that occurred on the Lord's Day during Old Home Week.

"Lighten our darkness, we beseech Thee, O Lord; and by Thy great mercy defend us from all perils and dangers of this night; for the love of Thy only Son, our Saviour, Jesus Christ. Amen."

That solemn prayer and other similar ones were heard through out Pottsville as the evening church services in all the houses of worship were formally commemorating the founding of the town; with raucous celebrations set to officially begin at the stroke of midnight. When ended, the crowds of churchgoers joined those who did not attend the liturgical ceremonies, and together they all proceeded downtown to the heart of Centre Street. Yes, it was raining outside but the light shower failed to dampen anyone's spirits. By eleven o'clock, one hour before the festivities were to begin, the swarm of celebrants was on the verge of being considered "uncontrollable" by some eyewitnesses. However order prevailed that night of nights.

At approximately 11:30 P.M. the rain lessened to merely a nuisance drizzle, and at the stroke of midnight, the electrical current for the decorative illuminations, all strung up high along the streets, was switched on. Along Centre Street, as well as the adjoining streets, the decorations brightened the night sky, dazzling the multitudes that have gathered, almost as if you could hear one mighty, collective and wondrous "*Aah*" coming from the community.

"Yahoo! Yahoo! Yahoo!"

"Whoopee!"

"Harrah!"

"Hip Hip Hurray!"

The shrieks of celebration from the estimated crowd of 30,000 quickly filled the moist air, accompanied by the clanging of cowbells and other merriment makers.

At that same instant, the melodious Third Brigade Band appeared on Centre Street, marching in perfect step formation forward to the Centennial Committee's Headquarters.

"Forward! March! One, two, three, four! One, two, three, four!"

Look out world! The celebrations had officially begun!

The Third Brigade Band, in full blue uniform, triumphantly headed towards Garfield Square, accompanied by approximately twenty-five "lamp boys" who carried the illumination permitting the musicians to read their sheet music. Some of the lads were wet and disheveled from the light rain, reminding some passersby of "breaker boys"—those youngsters who sorted the coal from the rock as it flowed down the chutes at the nearby collieries. To be picked as "a lamp boy" for the centennial celebration was indeed a great honor, and these boys were very proud to be selected, despite the ragged appearances of many of them, now wet with the fallen rain and coated with the dust from the streets.

Boys will be boys, whether it was 1906 or 1955.

Located five blocks west of Centre Street, this town square, re-named after President James Garfield, served as the center of most patriotic celebrations since 1891, the year when the Soldiers and Sailors Monument was erected to honor the local military heroes. The Band, in the glow provided by the energetic lamp boys, continued to the Square, playing one upbeat march after another. The crowds along the way, unremittingly cheer, clap and holler.

"Pottsville is one hundred years young!"

"Hip! Hip! Hurray!"

Professor Frederic Gerhard was the brilliant conductor of the beloved Third Brigade Band that was a part of Pottsville's one hundred year old history. In 1864, this handsome and rugged musician was born at Hummelstown, a Pennsylvania Dutch town located near the state capital of Harrisburg. His early years had been spent in the northern parts of Schuylkill County.

In 1875, young Fred could be spotted as a black-faced, begrimed breaker boy living outside of Shenandoah. Where he got his first violin, no one knows, but he could be seen practicing the dainty instrument, with his slate bruised hands, after his hours of long hard labor. At age nineteen, he came to Pottsville and began employment in the foundry of the Philadelphia and Reading Coal & Iron Company. While working those long hours, he never took his mind off of his true passion and his unfulfilled aspirations, that of becoming an accomplished musician and a conductor of classical compositions.

In his evenings Gerhard devoted himself to this true love, the study of music. When he thought he was at least competent, he began playing in several local theatre orchestras. His musical talent astounded nearly everyone that had heard him. Soon he made a decision to leave the foundry, plunging himself into the new world of his dreams. He would be a professional musician, and strive to become the finest in all of Pottsville and its neighboring towns and villages. It certainly took courage to make that decision and give up his job security. By 1906 it is apparent that he has fulfilled his childhood dream.

"I will prove my talent to the world and make the most beautiful music that Pottsville has ever or will ever hear," Gerhard would repeatedly tell his friends and relatives, who all believed in him.

In 1889, Gerhard traveled to New York City where he spent a year studying music theory, playing the violin under the tutelage of Dr. Eugene Thayer (an early American organ virtuoso and composer of organ music), and Gustav Dannreuther, founder of the Beethoven String Quartet. All the while he longed to return to his beloved Pottsville, as the big city life was not for him.

After his homecoming to the coal region the following year, he was elected leader of the Third Brigade Band, which was founded in 1879 as a military band, and composed entirely of Pottsville men. Besides acting as its leader, Professor Gerhard organized his symphony orchestra as well as a string quartet. In order to support himself, he spends considerable time instructing students in piano and violin. Having music lessons taught by Gerhard quickly became a status symbol to the local population. "Lessons by Gerhard" meant first-class musical education.

"That was a little clumsy, but if you practice at least one hour every day, you will master the first movement of the Mozart G minor," Gerhard could be heard telling many a student, firmly believing that practice, practice and more practice made perfect.

On the streets of Pottsville, the energetic musicians, collectively known as the "Third Brigade Band," now marching in perfect unison for the opening celebration had appeared in numerous historic events over the years. For instance, during the Homestead Strike of 1892, the band entertained the National Guard that was stationed outside of Pittsburgh. The Guard was sent there by Governor Patterson to keep peace between the strikers and the management. After their departure from the camp, the band visited the office of Henry C. Frick, the fabulously wealthy coke king and steel magnate where they played a musical number for him. Shortly after the Pottsville band serenaded him, an attempt was made on Frick's life, resulting in a serious, but non-fatal, gunshot wound. The would-be assassin was Alexander Berkman, the partner and lover of the notorious anarchist, Emma Goldman. Berkman had been wrestled to the ground, and his captors noticed that his face appeared suspicious.

"Open your mouth! What do you have in your jaw?"

"Candy," Berkman defiantly answered.

After the prisoner was properly secured, it was discovered that Berkman had a dynamite cartridge in his mouth.

On their way back to Pottsville, the band members, who had avoided the attempted assassination by minutes, were startled to hear about the terrible gas explosion that occurred in their neighboring Yorkville. The deadly blast claimed the lives of several friends, and neighbors, and the musicians immediately volunteered their services at the funerals.

Yes, the Third Brigade Band become, over time, the historic heartbeat of Pottsville. This heartbeat was heard at many joyous occasions outside of Pottsville and Schuylkill County as well, making the band Pottsville's ambassadors of goodwill. Many astute followers of the band say that their finest playing was heard at the numerous inaugurations of American Presidents and Pennsylvania governors.

On Sunday night, the beginning of the most joyous of times in the town's history, Gerhard proudly performed a march composed by one of his most prized pupils, his nephew Robert Brown. Robert, along with his younger brother and their father, a widowed physician, boarded with Professor Gerhard for over ten years. Great indebtedness was owed to his uncle Frederic for both Brown's early inspiration and the many musical lessons given to him. Under the professor's careful eye, Robert studied both violin and piano. Day in and day out, the determined Robert practiced his Beethoven sonatas, resulting in his being hailed as a child protégé at the tender age of eleven. He was considered Pottsville's boy wonder.

The town would never witness such a musical genius in its midst ever again.

When the Third Brigade Band reached the town square, the Pottsville Liederkranz waited in anticipation of joining in with a night of German songs and merriment.

"Wenn das Band ankommt, verbinden wir sie in der Musik!" yelled the orchestra leader to his anxious disciples.

The Liederkranz prided itself as being one of the oldest social clubs in the city, and was devoted to preservation of "High German" culture. This orchestra also featured a most distinguished bandleader in the name of Professor Rudolph Haussman, a graduate of the conservatory of music in Prague, fluent in six European languages. The Professor's impressive resume included eighteen months as a member of the Johann Strauss Orchestra. In 1906, he devoted all of his energy and talent on his adopted Pottsville.

While all of the town's musicians were coming together at the Square, other unusual shenanigans were taking place.

"There he is boys! Let's take him in. Don't let him get away!" While these words were spoken, there was no sense of alarm and no crime was being committed. At the square, the centennial committee ceremoniously captured Pottsville's Chief Burgess, Edwin Stine, thereby "seizing control" of the town. The Burgess was required to authorize a permit giving the Committee the right to rule the town until "the dawn's early light." "The Burgess" was the central figure in the town's government, as Pottsville did not yet have a mayor due to the City Charter movement, having been defeated once again in 1905, but by only 45 votes that time. These electoral attempts were getting closer, so it would be only a matter of time before those clamoring for change could claim victory.

"The system is holding up progress, and the only progress being made is by those who hold influence and power. It's time for a real change!"

Critics of the current governmental system argued that the burgess was nothing more than a glorified clerk who issued permits for construction, circuses and parades. Furthermore, his only official duty was to reorganize council annually. A council of twenty-two men was also too cumbersome. The critics held that the tax collector and the treasurer conducted the real business of the borough without much oversight; the checks on graft and corruption were minimal. The supporters, on the other hand, held an opposing position, claiming that the burgess system was working fine in the town, and any attempt to alter the status quo would result in skyrocketing real estate taxes and rents.

"A city charter is basically anti-business and anti-property owner!"

Edwin S. Stine was the youngest Burgess in the history of Pottsville, elected in February of the centennial year at the age of twenty-nine. After completing high school he worked for three years in the restaurant business at the Tumbling Run Hotel in the nearby resort area before getting a political job as clerk for the County Commissioners. He won the election as a minority burgess, as he failed to gain 50% of the vote total. However, it appeared that the citizens were now tiring of the current system, and the charter movement was steadily gaining in popularity. On Sunday night, the Committee stripped the Burgess of whatever authority he had and the people ruled.

"This week the people rule!"

The multitude of people that filled the streets appeared to represent the entire current population, along with the myriad of former residents and visitors who came to Pottsville for the week of revelry. These outsiders came mainly by locomotive. The sprawling and imposing "Queen Anne" style depot, constructed by the Philadelphia & Reading Railroad located at Railroad and Norwegian Street, had been open to the public since 1887. With the influx of the early trains on Saturday evening, the visitors arrived non-stop. The P & R "Flyer," an express passenger train, arrived from Philadelphia, filling to capacity its twelve cars. The arrival of the numerous trains created a steady stream of people traveling from the station to several hotels or the homes of relatives and friends. At the station one saw every character of human beings in one place. At no time in its one hundred year history did the town have such a crowd of people surging about.

The revelers included many teenagers, including young George Simon, Jr., from the east side, and a girl, slightly older than him, from the west side, sweet-faced Viola Hartranft. George's father was a machinist who worked in the Village of Delano, located approximately sixteen miles north of Pottsville. The Simons' lived on North George Street, a quiet, hilly residential neighborhood. George was the darling of his parents, both of whom had made a fuss over their son, making sure that his material needs, as well as his material wishes were taken care of. His desire that night was to take part in the town's centennial festivities, together with his beloved Viola. To George, this relationship represented more than a first "puppy love" as the young lad desired to marry Viola. He could not wait to graduate from high school. But on this night of nights, with everyone wandering about on these wildly illuminated streets, his mind was not on marriage, but on Pottsville's glorious history and its hopeful future. There was no curfew that night; no need to fear the dreaded bull whistle that sounds at nine o'clock, signaling the hour for all children to be in their homes and off the streets.

For the most part, the crowd was dressed in "Sunday's finest." 1906 was considered part of the Edwardian era in the fashion world. If you looked down at numerous feet shuffling about, then you saw the high-buttoned shoes of the day on both men and women. Occasionally you saw shoes fastened with laces but for the most part button shoes were worn. Every household had a buttoner, a small bar with a hook shaped end that permitted the wearer to insert the button hook into the eyelet, grasping the button, then drawing it into its proper position to close the shoe. Most of the women and older girls wore cotton stockings, either black or white. Most of the shoes were black in 1906 with an occasional brown showing up. Men also wore cotton stockings with a garter girding the calf of the leg to hold them up. There were a lot of feet moving about the streets of town that night.

The idealized woman at this time was "a Gibson girl"—tall, artful, stately, and superbly dressed. The Gibson girl was a tiny-waisted, hourglass shaped, delicate figure. Her crowning glory was a lady's hat—garnished with lace, yards of ribbon, fruit, feathers or flowers; most evening hats were made of velvet and silk. This period, prior to World War I, was a time of extravagance, and it showed in women's fashion.

Only young girls wore short dresses. Once a girl reached high school age she donned a long ankle length dress with a rustling petticoat underneath. Indeed, there was a lot of rustling being heard that night, just listen.

Boys and young men wore three-piece suits for dress or evening, normally consisting of coat, vest and knee pants, which were tight fitting. The shirts were generally made of cotton flannel with detachable collars and cuffs. Of course, all of the men wore hats, and straw hats had become popular than the silk hats, the latter now worn for more formal occasions. Whatever type of hat was worn, no gentleman would be seen on a public street with his head uncovered.

Soon a great aerial fireworks display high atop Lawton's Hill, on the eastern side of town, was set off, adding to the radiance provided to the downtown by the more than 5,000 electric lights strung up high over the streets.

The glowing embers of color slowly tumbled in the night air mesmerizing all those who watched.

"Look! Oh, how beautiful!"

Everywhere around town, the innumerable, lighted Chinese lanterns added a stylish touch. George Simon, as well as many other young lovers, did not appreciate the powerful spotlights, shining down from atop the Morris Building placed there by the town's largest department store. It seemed as if the lights followed you around. As most young couples, George wanted time alone with his heart's desire; he did not want to be under the watchful glare of a spotlight. Some of the old timers were up on the rooftop, moving the spotlight around, spying on the pedestrians down below. Young, romantic couples did not want to be watched, and were eager for the solitude that this night offers. They sought out the discreet shadows of the side streets.

"Turn that damn light off, will ya!"

"Let's walk over there; we will avoid the glare of the lights and the stare of the nosey."

"Weren't you ever young and in love once? The night should be for lovers."

When the sun rises over Lawton's Hill, the crowds had mostly dispersed; sleep was needed, as the gigantic Labor Day Parade was scheduled to start at eleven o'clock. Yes, by now most wanted the comfort of being wrapped in the comfort of a blanket of sleep. Soon, the sun's welcome rays of warmth would dry away the dampness of the night, and strengthen those hearty or foolish enough to remain up all night, including one youthful poet reciting a verse to his maiden companion.

"Sleep, Sleep, beauty bright,
Dreaming in the joys of night,
Sleep, sleep; in thy sleep,
Little sorrows sit and weep."

—William Blake

CHAPTER 3

▼

LABOR DAY
CELEBRATIONS

Are you familiar with the history of labor unions in this country? Why, much of their history began in earnest in Schuylkill County during the 19th century. There was one early episode that occurred in 1842, when a group of miners and laborers from Minersville marched into Pottsville to present a list of grievances to their employers. I understand that they were somewhat unruly, and when they appeared in Pottsville on a Sunday afternoon, the citizens of Pottsville, startled by the appearance of the men, some with carrying clubs in their hands and many covered with coal grime and soot, chased them away.

Things slowly improved for the working class as the decades proceeded, and by 1906 union members were welcomed with open arms in Pottsville.

From the cupola, or roof-top look-out, the conductor gave his signal as his powerful steam engine train approached the station house.

"Next stop, Potts-Ville, Penn-Sil-Vain-Nee-Yaw! Please watch your step when alighting from the car."

All morning long, the crowds poured into town by horse team, train and trolley. The first train arrived early at the Pennsylvania Station from the mining town of Shenandoah. The Pennsy, as the train station is commonly referred to, was an all-stone spacious building with a covered waiting platform, and a very busy transport hub. On a regular business day, thirty-four trains generally stopped at the Pennsy station. On Labor Day, the special run dropped off the many passengers who filled its eight cars that boarded in Shenandoah. Standing room only! The train was so crowded that a second trip was hastily arranged, necessary for those eager passengers unable to board when the scheduled train departed. That second train was also standing room only. It appeared that every engine entering the station was pulling extra passenger cars that Labor Day.

The Pennsy was not the only hectic depot in town, as just a short distance away, the "Queen Anne" style Reading Station was equally busy. Conductor Meiswinkle's Ashland train arrived with 1,500 passengers, setting a record. September 1906 was certainly a time for everyone to visit Pottsville and join in the celebration.

It seemed that all types of humanity were rubbing elbows that week—the miners, bankers, coal barons, servants, con artists, farmers, doctors, streetwalkers, and school children. Name a group, and that group was present somewhere in Pottsville. They assembled for the anticipated "party of the century" being hosted by the townspeople. The organizing committee christened the event "Old Home Week," and the word had been sent out, near and far, that anyone who has connections with Pottsville should return for the festivities.

"I think I saw that young Jack Picus in town. He's probably home to visit his family and join in the celebrations. Boy can he throw that baseball."

Voices in the crowd spread the word that Jack Picus had come back for Old Home Week. He was the young foreigner who was hoping to earn a place on a major league baseball team. *Foreigner* was the term given primarily to those of eastern or southern European ancestry.

"The major leagues will chew him up."

As for his talent, Jack Picus could dream couldn't he? He had played good ball on the back lots of the Mount Hope section of the town; well enough to play with various amateur local teams.

"What an incredible spitball that young man could throw! Maybe he would later play a game or two at Tumbling Run."

Yes, Jack had returned home, to celebrate with everyone else, proudly watching the biggest and best parade that was ever held in the region—the Labor Day Parade of Old Home Week.

That parade kicked off on Monday morning, right on schedule, with the fire whistle blowing loudly at eleven o'clock. The energetic Third Brigade Band headed the parade, played inspiring familiar marches as well as many of the newer ones composed by John Philip Sousa.

"How many people are packed on the street? I feel like a sardine!"

The crowds pushed forward to the edge of the sidewalks with everyone attempting to get a good view, difficult in that era as everyone had a hat one.

Looking around, no one was able to count the number of on-lookers accurately, but the various newspapers estimated that the visitors swelled the population from ten thousand to seventy five thousand. Besides the trainloads of passengers, the arriving guests came from other localities by foot, horseback, trolley, and automobile.

C.P. Hoffman, the Centennial chairman, looking proud as a peacock that morning, rode his stallion down the street as he followed behind the band.

"Good morning, ladies, I hope you enjoy the parade," he politely told a group of young girls standing along Centre Street.

Immediately behind Mr. Hoffman came the numerous labor leaders from the county with the workingmen and women following in formation. Bands of musicians were interspersed with these marchers, giving the parade a true celebratory atmosphere.

The First Lithuanian Band of Shenandoah, consisting of thirty musicians, many of who were coal miners and members of the local United Mine Workers #300, was the second band to march. The band proudly displayed a large banner, "United We Stand, Divided We Fall" evidencing its commitment to the struggles of organized labor.

In 1900 and 1902 this band, under the direction of its Greek born conductor, Arthur Grimes, was instrumental in boosting the moral of the striking anthracite coal miners and their families during the economic hard times. Their reputation for brilliance was so widespread, the musicians were able to raise several thousands of dollars to support the striking miners by performing in New York City concert halls. When the Great Strike of 1902 ended in October of that year, First Lithuanian Band of Shenandoah triumphantly led the large victory parade around Shenandoah. Today they would salute Pottsville on its one-hundredth birthday.

"Sveikinu su gimtadieniu," the Shenandoah marchers cheerfully told the countless onlookers in their native tongue. To those fluent in Lithuanian, the translation was "Happy Birthday!"

The Carpenter's Union soon followed with one hundred fifty men, all dressed in pressed black trousers and crisp, clean white shirts. The stream of workers, which included many women, in many instances, sang along with the various marching bands from the other coal region towns, such as Minersville and Shamokin. They were all marching together—the Typographical Union, the Cigar Workers Union with a banner proclaiming, "We are opposed to child labor!"

The Iron Molders Union, the Masons, the Eastern Steel Company workers, and all of the others representing the working class, of not only Pottsville, but also the whole county, followed the Cigar Workers. The steelworker contingent filled three-square blocks with all of the employees dressed in angelic white. It was quite an impressive spectacle.

The marching employees of the Tilt Silk Mills who followed were well received by those on the reviewing stands and sidewalks. The Silk Mill, located at Twelfth Street, was one of the town's largest employers. The crowd, drenched by the confetti that rained down from the rooftops of the downtown stores, was delighted to be part of Pottsville's glorious birthday celebration, even if they had to stand for hours for not paying the twenty five cents necessary to have a grand-stand seat.

"How do we get out of here?" asked several exhausted spectators as the last contingent of workingmen strutted by.

The parade was completed without any hitch, and now those on the streets fumbled through the crushing humanity to the various destinations. Many of the spectators as well as participants went to relax at nearby Tumbling Run Park, which was conveniently located a short trolley car away from the downtown. At the park numerous boathouses were all thematically decorated. The best-decorated boathouse would receive the grand prize of fifteen dollars. That was a lot of money in 1906, and the competition was fierce. Swimming and diving competitions followed throughout the day. By evening, the electric lights illuminated the boathouses, and the beauty was hard to describe by those unaccustomed to the wonders of electricity. Gaily colored lanterns bedecked the many boats out on the water, and the strains of sweet music, both vocal and instrumental, filtered the shouts of happiness, the merry laughter and hum of the conversations heard on the shoreline.

For those that did not venture out to Tumbling Run, taking in the sights and sounds of downtown Pottsville served as the main activity. Many indulged in impromptu parading and revelry in the streets and on the sidewalks. The downtown overflowed with the various sidewalk shows and special attractions, all carefully planned with the idea of the special entertainment continuing throughout the early evening. The deep loud voice of the carnival barker could be heard for almost a block away.

"Step right up gentlemen, She wiggles, She giggles, She talks, She walks!"

On one corner, the colorful barker enticed the men to venture into his tent that featured the exotic "Serpentine Girl," and nearby was a mustached, Italian organ-grinder entertaining his audience with his trained monkey. His bellowing tenor voice was heard for a half a block, bellowing "Santa Lucia" and other native songs. The excited monkey, held on a chain by his owner, dressed in a red vest and matching fez hat, held a lively white rat, and at times the ring tailed primate seemed to juggle the rodent to the delight of numerous onlookers, or the fears of many of the fairer sex, who appeared to be suffering from musophobia—the fear of mice.

"Eiwe! Let's get away from that monkey! Do you see what he has in his hands? Eiwe!"

Further to the west, Garfield Square was filled with midway tents and fakirs of every stripe, as well as hosting a fairly large Ferris wheel, one of two in Pottsville that week.

"Mama! Can we please ride one more time! Please mama, please."

The effect that a carnival has on children has never changed over time.

The newspapers all agreed that the centennial celebration was a huge success, with splendid time being had by all. The Pottsville police had made sure that lawlessness did not overtake the festivities. Only a few incidents deserved police attention. Yes, there were numerous saloon fights but the police quickly broke up the scuffles, dragging the participants through the town without further incident. On the Saturday prior to the celebration, the chief had issued a stern warning that the police would push all suspicious characters to the limit and arrested without a warrant. For the most part, his warning is being heeded.

"No acts of violence, indecency, or general misconduct will be tolerated. Any desecration of the Sabbath and any interference with evening church services will result in an immediate arrest. The town will not be given over to the pluguglies, thieves, drunks and rowdies. The celebration is for the people, including women and children."

The only known serious offense occurred when a quarrel erupted between two men in Howell's East Norwegian Street saloon. The barkeep urgently summoned the police on his telephone, as he needed help right away.

"There is a wild *I-talian* in the bar and he is out of control, waving a big stiletto knife around. I want him out of here before he hurts someone!"

Chief of Police Hiram Davies rode over in his police car, subduing the irate customer, placing him under arrest, and removing him to the station for lock-up.

When he opened the jail cell door, the aggressive prisoner stepped back and attempted to jump the Chief.

"Just try that again! Take that!"

Davies was too quick for him, delivering one stunning punch to his would-be attacker's jaw. The troublemaker fell back against the wall, and while dazed, placed into the holding cell by the no-nonsense police chief. The next day Davies proudly displayed his colorfully bruised left thumb caused by his single punch. He showed it off as a badge of honor in protecting Pottsville that centennial year.

Included in the throng of partygoers that day was a young couple, Dr. Patrick O'Hara and his wife, Katherine. The Shenandoah physician had married his bride three years ago in Lykens, which lies over the western edge of the county line. The newlywed couple had settled at 125 Mahantongo Street in a three-story brick and wood house across the street from the Academy of Music, the cultural center of the coal region that features symphony orchestras, opera and professional theatre productions.

The Academy of Music opened to the public on January 17, 1876 with a production of Shakespeare's "Macbeth." Not a bad start for a theatre in a small coal town. The show palace had 1,382 tilted, scarlet plush velvet seats. Pure white, columned tiers added the necessary support; the ceiling was painted with panels and ornaments on gold grounds. The main panels depicted the Greek muses and the goddesses of dance, comedy, and tragedy. The minor panels depicted the seasons and also celebrated composers. Lighting was supplied by the main reflecting chandeliers with fifty gas burners and the lower branches holding thirty burners. The huge stage was dressed with a curtain that was a piece of artwork in its own right, depicting St. Goar on the Rhine. All of the New York shows came to the Academy, not just summer stock productions, but first-run production companies.

Greek tragedies could be seen at the Theatre on occasion, but it is uncertain if the story of *Orestes* was ever performed there. Orestes was the character that killed his own mother, *Clytaimestra*. He was punished for the vile matricide by being driven mad by the Furies. These mythological figures were goddesses of vengence, and were horrible to look at. Often they were depicted as repulsive, winged female creatures, dressed in long black robes. Others described the Furies as being adorned with snakes twined in their hair, piercing red eyes dripping blood, pitch-black bodies with bat wings, and even sporting the heads of dogs. The Furies punished criminals, especially murderers. They acted on complaints and punished the transgressors, relentlessly hounding the culprits. Nobody could escape from the Furies' wrath—they pursued their victims from city to city and country to country, without rest or pause. They would strike the offenders with madness and never stopped following criminals. The worst of all crimes were patricide or matricide, and first and foremost, the Furies would punish this kind of crime. The Furies became the personification of the concepts of vindictiveness and retribution and represented the psychological torments associated with a guilty conscience. *Orestes* is a most interesting story.

Greek mythology and culture was studied at Pottsville High School, as no education was complete without basic knowledge of these ancient stories. Studying these tales enhanced a child's imagination, while simultaneously sharpening reading, writing and speaking skills. Many young scholars loved the adventurous depictions of the Greek heroes, heroines, beasts and villains. The Academy of Music offered an opportunity for a few of these stories to come to life. For an hour or two, a stage production made the various gods, goddesses and furies all so real. Mythology and Fable have always had a role in telling the story of humanity and it was no different in Pottsville, Pennsylvania.

Back on Mahantongo Street, Dr. O'Hara was outside watching some of the Labor Day festivities with his 20 month-old son, John. Patrick was an up and coming surgeon who had recently returned from studying modern surgery in Germany, Austria and England. The young family resided in the upper floor of the building which housed his office and operating room. His patients crossed the social strata of Pottsville, and included the wealthy as well as the recent eastern and southern impoverished European immigrants. His home office was a most convenient place for a home delivery. In fact, John, the doctor's first-born son, was one of the earliest deliveries on the premises. The house stood at the base of Mahantongo Street, which, for sixteen blocks, featured the homes resided in by many of the town's remaining aristocracy, as well being the location of the headquarters of the powerful Philadelphia & Reading Coal & Iron Company. In the rear of the office, the young doctor, who was an avid equestrian, maintained a stable for his several horses. He would teach his son the art of horseback riding when the boy was a little older. Horses were still very popular, and many thought that the automobile would never replace them as automobiles were too expensive for the average family. Looking in the Business Directory, one would see that Pottsville was the home of eleven blacksmiths, so horsepower was still the favored means of transportation. The young surgeon would not ride his horse that Labor Day as the streets were too crowded with excitable people and horses, even those well-trained, could be easily frightened.

At that moment, George Simon, Viola and several other adolescents passed by.

"Good afternoon, doc."

"Good afternoon. It was a spectacular parade, wasn't it?"

"It sure was. It will be hard to beat. Anyway, we won't be around for the bicentennial."

CHAPTER 4

▼

MAHANTONGO STREET

John O'Hara got his start with the Miners Journal. That author is pretty much a persona non grata in Pottsville. I have that in common with him, as well as the love of a good drink and a good story. Someday I am sure, long after he is dead, a marker or two will be put up and everyone in the town will fawn all over him, while my remains will be donated to the University of Pennsylvania for medical research and there will be no trace of my existence to be found. No one will acknowledge that he or she even knew me. I truly will be gone and forgotten. A person is better off not reflecting upon the meaning of existence. The world is less mysterious and complicated to those who don't think. At least, that is my opinion. I envy those people. Anyway, the street that O'Hara lived on truly was a special little world.

Three blocks up the street from Doc O'Hara's home was the "Yuengling Brewery," a prominent business that proudly advertised its famous malt beverage with the following remarks: *"It's a tonic!" "It's nourishing!" "It's wholesome!" ""It's invigorating!" "It's endorsed by physicians!" "It creates better appetites!" "It contains valuable food properties!" "It aids digestion!"* Notwithstanding all of this advertising, the beer gained widespread popularity throughout the county, primarily due to its good taste. The brewery owner, young Mr. Frank Yuengling, took over the family business at the age of 22 in 1899, upon the unexpected death of his father. Frank proved to be an able and determined manager, and the brewery continued to thrive. Production reached 65,000 barrels in 1900. This was the golden age of

American brewing, as a record number of 2,156 breweries operated throughout the nation, with Pottsville having two presently; the second was Rettig's Brewery, at Ninth and West Market Street.

Young Frank Yuengling continues to manage the family brewery to this very day. The name Yuengling would eventually become synonymous with Pottsville itself.

Mahantongo Street definitely possessed a chic cosmopolitan atmosphere, clearly obvious whenever one strolled up its hill. If you were heading to St. Patrick's Church or the neighboring Yuengling Brewery, you would first pass the solidly constructed townhouses, neatly arranged side by side. Miss Sarah A. McCool, a schoolteacher and noted historian, lived in one of the homes. She just passed away a few months earlier. Pity that she did not live long enough to enjoy the historic centennial festivities. After the brewery, continuing westward, one would discover the elaborate mansion houses with their tidy green lawns, conservatories filled with exotic plants, separate servant quarters, and stables housing thoroughbreds and trotters. The wealth found along Mahantongo Street irritated some. In fact, Dr. O'Hara's son would evolve professionally into a social critic of the mores and idiosyncrasies of the elite that resided on his street. He would make this street legendary within the literary world, winning a National Book Award along the way.

Many of these homes contained their own little histories. Oh, if some of the walls talked, you'd be mesmerized by the stories that you would hear. For instance, a James Gillingham lived at 622 Mahantongo St. This gentleman was a member of the Society of Friends, better known as the Quakers, who had been an active station keeper in the Underground Railroad network, helping escaped slaves find freedom in the northern states and Canada. Yes, that house holds a history all of its own, as do many others, but the Gillingham story is one of my favorites.

Not all of the Pottsville wealthy lived on Mahantongo Street, but it certainly contained more financially well-to-do persons per square foot within the town, or even the county at that time.

Burd Patterson was one of the first aristocrats to settle on the street in the early 1830s. His stately, beautiful house remained intact as one of the few vestiges of the 19th century glory days, while most of the others would see decline, neglect or demolition by the time Pottsville celebrated another one hundred years.

Most of the old moneyed people were scattered around the borough. For instance, Allan C. Milliken, the manager of the large Eastern Steel Company, constructed his large residence on the east side of Pottsville, far up Greenwood

Hill, past where young George Simon lived. Milliken lived there until his death in 1905, the year before the big centennial. Years later, his philanthropic widow, Alice, would convert the estate into the Anthracite Hospital. When the Spanish Flu epidemic of 1918 frightens Pottsville and the surrounding towns, Allan C. Milliken's widow, Alice, generously opens up her exquisite Greenwood Hill home to the sick, placing 50 hospital beds within for these patients. A true work of Christian charity, I must say. She permitted tents to be erected on her neatly groomed lawn, allowing the sick children a place of their own. Her generosity continued to grow, and the home will eventually be donated in 1929, as a permanent community hospital, to be named "the Good Samaritan Hospital." Alice Milliken will rightfully earn the praise of every resident and be fondly remembered as one of the town's most noble women.

In 1899 Allan and Alice Milliken's daughter, Anne, married James Barlow Cullum, a brilliant chemist and businessman. J. Barlow Cullum was a manufacturer of rock trap materials, which were used in the production of iron and steel. In the centennial year, Mr. Cullum purchased a palatial estate at 14th Street and Howard Avenue, at the western fringe of Pottsville. Mr. Cullum was an exceptionally shrewd investor, able to retire at the youthful age of thirty-seven as a very wealthy man. The Cullums, with their two children, had at least five live-in servants residing in their new home, nicknamed "White Lodge." The dwelling, erected in the 1870s by Colonel John E. Wynkoop, was reputed to be the grandest home in all of Pottsville. Mr. Cullum purchased the premises for his wife from a subsequent owner, Mrs. William Fox.

Anne Milliken Cullum desired a residence closer to her parents. Unfortunately her father died in 1905, just prior to the centennial year, survived by his widow, Alice, who remained at the Greenwood Hill home. The Cullums already owned a beautiful home in Pittsburgh, and placed it under long-term lease, as they intended to reside in Pottsville in between their scheduled extended European vacations.

Their Pottsville home has an extensive event-filled history, and was undoubtedly one of the best known of the upper class homes in the town; the center for more parties and social functions that any other property in Pottsville. Colonel Wynkoop was known for his love of parties, as was his successor, Mrs. Fox. It had a magnificent ballroom, surrounded by spacious porches that overlook the extensive and well-manicured grounds. The Cullums intended to maintain the tradition and keep the house in the social pages for years to come.

Four blocks west of the Cullum mansion was the quarters of The Outdoor Club, which recently received its charter. This social center was reached by walking up the boardwalk leading up from Eighteenth Street. Operating mainly as a private tennis club, the club had handsome quarters providing a delightful site where tennis teas, informal dances, and afternoon parties were held for the prosperous of the community. Many of the social elite belonged to this club, with names such as Wilhelm, Carpenter, Farquhar, Bechtel and Schaeffer on its membership roster. Later, as golf became increasingly more popular with the patricians, the Outdoor Club would fade into history, replaced by the Schuylkill County Club, which operates to this day.

Pottsville's aristocracy was already on the decline during the centennial year, although this fact was not blatantly obvious. Money, and lots of money, was still being made, but not in the amounts seen in the 19th century. The recession of the 1870s dealt a great blow to the town, but its effects were largely unseen to the common eye. Yet Mahantongo Street would remain part of the town's folklore. It would always remain somewhat of an illusion of the great glory days of Pottsville's past. The sons and daughters of the original upper-class settlers were already leaving the area in large numbers, seeking opportunities elsewhere. In the coming decades most of the aristocratic families will relocate to other parts of the country. The approaching federal income tax will also chip away at their family fortunes. But now Pottsville was holding its centennial, and it was time to celebrate.

CHAPTER 5

▼

THE PARTY CONTINUES

The first school was erected in Pottsville, supposedly in 1811 in the "Reep Church,"
later known as the "Dutch Church." An old soldier, who was formerly in the German
Cavalry, ran the school. Everyone in the school had to speak German. I find German
to be an ugly language; when spoken it sounds as if the person was sick to his stomach.
   As for me, I graduated from Pottsville High School, the first in my family to get a
diploma. The public high school was started in 1853, and my principal was Reverend
Patterson. He probably stood at the top of the list of Pennsylvania educator. He passed
away during the centennial year
   Overall, I had to unlearn many of the things that I was taught in school.

On Tuesday, the day after the big parade, the downtown hosted the Civic
Parade that featured marching bands, civic clubs and the many floats constructed
by local merchants. The Third Brigade Band led the Odd Fellows, the Knights of
Malta, the Italian Society, the Knights of the Golden Eagle, the Liederkranz, as
well as other clubs, too numerous to remember.

Behind these organizations of people came the beautiful floats. Horses were
pulling the float of Dives, Pomeroy and Stewart, which depicted a large Oxford
shoe. The women and children that worked at the large department store followed in several horse drawn coaches; the women were all dressed in white, holding white parasols, waving to those on the sidewalks. Other floats featured player
pianos, sewing machines, kitchen cabinets and carpeting. This parade represented

a middle class consumer's fantasy of the appliances and items that lessen the workload of running a household and make daily living more enjoyable.

On Wednesday, the grand Military-Firemen Parade began at 2 P.M., before a crowd estimated at 50,000. No one seemed to tire of watching another parade. Sprinkled between the marching bands were all of the fire trucks and wagons that represent the best of the coal region. James Lynaugh, delighted to participate and show off the latest equipment being used in the town, was the town fire chief. Visiting departments included Columbia Hose Company of Shenandoah, Mountaineer of Minersville and Friendship of Orwigsburg. The Columbia Hose Company was followed by its Boys Cadet Band of thirty five young musicians, all in short trousers, crisp white shirts and blue caps. They created quite an impression, receiving a thunderous applause as they passed by. As fire was the greatest danger to the populace, the townspeople had enormous pride and respect for their protectors, and the vocal cheers wildly expressed these emotions as each fire brigade proceeded by.

Mr. and Mrs. Cullum left their Howard Avenue estate to watch the parade and cheer the military and the firemen as they marched by. In six months the Cullum family would have special reason to be grateful to the firemen, but on this day they had no forewarning of what the future held for them.

Union veterans of the Civil War and the Spanish American War led the military contingents before the reviewing stand and the watchful eye of Generals Gobin and Governor Pennypacker. Yes, the distinguished guest of honor was, none other than, General John Peter Shindel Gobin, of Lebanon County, a military leader with an illustrious past. He had been a Civil War hero who participated in the capture of Jacksonville, Florida and the capture of the Confederate Steamer "Governor Milton," the only steamer captured by infantry during the war.

Gobin's post-civil war accomplishments included leading the Pennsylvania National Guard in actions against railroad and coal miner strikes, and civil unrest caused by the "Molly Maguires". During the Homestead Strike, he was there listening to the Third Brigade Band play for his soldiers. He had been elected a state senator in 1885, before reaching his pinnacle of his political career in 1899, when he was elected Lieutenant Governor of Pennsylvania, serving one term until 1903.

Besides his activities during the Molly era, Gobin's other actions in the county were quite remarkable. In 1902, the general had been called into action when violence erupted in Shenandoah during the anthracite coal strike. By that year, politics had no longer interested him, and he desired to resurrect his military career. Leading his troops on horseback invigorated him more than the ceremonial, boring task of being Lieutenant Governor. He and his troops arrived in Shenandoah on July 31st when the National Guard had been called upon to suppress the deadly riot that had erupted. Joe Beddall, a local hardware store owner, had been brutally murdered at the Reading Railroad Station.

When he arrived in Shenandoah, the General had informed the press that Shenandoah's town council appallingly refused to act in the crisis. He further stated that as Shenandoah police were so badly injured, and the citizens of Shenandoah had refused to volunteer to conduct the business of government, he was now in command. Shenandoah would remain under his authority and jurisdiction. His men had strict orders to keep the peace. They had every right to shoot to kill if necessary (and indeed they did shoot and they did kill). His command echoed up and down every street and alleyway of the mining community. Martial law was in effect, authorizing General Gobin to rule Shenandoah for several months.

On this centennial day, the controversial military officer returned once again to Schuylkill County. He was now the commander of the Third Brigade of the Pennsylvania National Guard, but this time he was there, neither to suppress the Molly Maguires, nor to administer martial law in Shenandoah. He was there to preside over the largest military parade in the county's history and listen to the music of the Third Brigade Band, as he especially loved to hear their renditions of the Sousa marches that were so popular. The General was in Pottsville to party along with the tens of thousands of other people. His only decree was for everyone to have a good time and behave him or herself.

That same evening, the town was entertained by the large "Mardi Gras" parade led by the its Elks Club. Leading the parade was a brand new automobile, or, as the old-timers say, a horseless carriage. Upon its hood was draped an elks head with ribbons flowing over the sides, each held by members of the Lodge. Every member was smartly dressed in a famous opera outfit; designed in Philadelphia at an enormous expense to the local club. While called a Mardi Gras by the organizing committee, the event actually resembled the feathery Mummer's Parade that graces the streets of Philadelphia every New Year's Day. Many in the crowds were heard commenting on the androgynous and humorous appearances of the elk members as the marchers all wore long flowing wigs, as they followed behind the exalted Elk Marshall, H.H. Seltzer.

Every single club in Pottsville joined in the revelry, including the Masonic Pulaski Lodge with its large group of members, led by their Worshipful Master,

William Pugh. The Lodge was the second oldest in the county having over two hundred members in 1906. The Lodge, located on the third floor of the Pennsylvania Bank Building, had a tidy treasury of its own. When opened in 1873, the Lodge was decorated with many exquisite frescoes; beautifully furnished at a cost estimated at six thousand dollars. It remained one of the most attractive club-houses or meeting rooms in all of Pottsville.

The crowds had not lessened, as people continued to pour into town by horse, train and trolley. Word kept spreading that Pottsville was the place to be. Such a joyous time to be alive! Everyone wanted to join in the revelry, celebrating the great honors being bestowed up the town.

The last parade was the Children's Parade that was postponed until Thursday, September 6th. All of the town's school children, from both the public and parochial schools, participated. For them it is a day off from the rigors of the McGuffey Reader, which contains the all too familiar short tales, verses, pronunciation and spelling lessons. Written in the 1830s and 1840s by university professor, William Holmes McGuffey, his books still remained the literary staple for countless schools throughout the nation.

The students marched through the downtown, accompanied by the energetic Third Brigade Band and the German Liederkranz orchestra. It was impossible to ascertain whether or not these men ever rested that week.

"My county 'tis of thee,
Sweet land of liberty,
Of thee I sing
Land where by fathers died!
Land of the pilgrims' pride!
From every mountainside
Let freedom ring!"

The children enthusiastically sang patriotic songs for the crowds that had gathered at Garfield Square. Such a wondrous time to be a young person in Pottsville that year! The large procession of children included George Simon, Helen Koch, Claude Lord, Joel Boone and so many others who eagerly anticipated the next hundred years in their community.The children celebrated along with adults, and they had much to celebrate as Pottsville showed so much promise.

"Move in a little closer. Say 'cheese.' Don't move! That's good, real good."

Many of the parents captured this moment in time with a brand new Kodak "brownie" camera that suddenly made its appearance as new gadget to play with.

All a person had to do is snap the shutter and there was a photograph of family members—in stiff but familiar poses that could be placed in the treasured family album.

"Ladies, Gentlemen and children of all ages! Welcome to the greatest show on earth! Come and see the E-lectrifying aerial act! Come to the big top!"

On Friday, the circus came to town. Whenever a circus visited Pottsville it brought delight to both young and old, but especially the young, who were treated to cotton candy, pop corn, and candied apples while the show was underway.

The train was late that evening due to a slight mishap on the track outside Tamaqua. As a result, the parade was very short and quick. The entertainment was advertised as "*W.L. Main's Circus and Cummins Wild West Show*" and it fulfilled the expectation of what every circus should have. There were "The Lady Zouaves Troupe of Arabian Acrobats," elephants, strong men, knife throwers, clowns and jugglers. Such a delight to see the joy in the eyes of the many children who clamored to their seats anxiously waiting for the greatest show on earth to begin.

While the children in the audience did not remember the tragedy of thirteen years ago, the elders certainly did. The Walter L. Main Circus was on the first leg of a tour through central Pennsylvania in May of 1893, when that horrible accident occurred. During the early morning hours of Memorial Day, the circus train was making its way down a long steep grade of the track, on its way from Clearfield to Tyrone in central Pennsylvania. The circus railroad cars were much longer and heavier than average railroad cars, and as the circus train reached the bottom of the hill, many cars containing circus animals and crew jumped the tracks. While many of the crew, performers and animals in the front of the train were spared, there were many people and animals in the back of the train injured and killed. Tyrone family lore, still recounted today, is the story of the escaped Bengal tiger. Several days after the wreck, a local farmer's daughter, Hannah Friday, was out milking her cow, when the escaped (and obviously hungry) tiger attacked and killed the cow. Hannah was able to escape the same fate, and a posse went out, found the tiger and shot it. Today, the tiger's skull hangs on the wall at the Tyrone Sportsman's Club. This certainly was no second rate circus, but rather one of the finest in the country. The circus was now in Pottsville to be the grand finale of the centennial celebration.

The second part of the entertainment, *Frederick T. Cummins' Wild West Show,* brought to town the famous Indian Chiefs, Indians from fifty-one tribes, cavalry and mounted 'armies' from around the world. This addition to the circus made the show a double-header; one that Pottsville would never forget. Red Chief, a revered Sioux warrior and second only in influence to Sitting Bull, arrived at the Pennsylvania Station, bedecked in war paint and feathers, anxious to perform the taming of the West for the Pottsville centennial celebrants. Red Chief had toured England and had performed for Queen Victoria, having impressed her enough that he is mentioned in her diary.

Now the Chief performed for the townspeople of Pottsville to close out glorious Old Home Week. It was certainly the perfect ending to a perfect week.

CHAPTER 6

▼

POLITICS

My dream was to become a great political journalist, and cover some of the national events, with Pottsville just being a stepping-stone for me. What I really wanted was to land a job with Joseph Pulitzer's New York World. That paper sponsored the trip around the world by Nellie Bly in 1899, and it also featured "The Yellow Kid," an early comic strip drawn by George Luks, the former Pottsville resident. You probably don't remember him. Yes, my goal was to get a job there in New York City. Pottsville was a good place to start and I loved Pottsville very much. I still do. There was a lot of politics to cover in those early days.

Politics in the coal region was just as rough and tumble as the football games. I really learned a lot. It was such a long time ago, but as soon as Old Home Week concluded, politics came to the forefront of everyone's attention.

The whole purpose of politics is to keep the population alarmed by instilling fears, mostly imaginary, in order that the people become anxious to be led to safety. That's the way it always was and always will be. That's just my opinion.

The autumn air crept into town, creating a palate of color on the street trees, while the centennial celebrations now fading into happy memories. Old Home Week would forever remain a highlight in Pottsville's History. Autumn's sweet, crisp smile returned the town's attention to the upcoming November national and state elections. Incumbent United States Representative Charles Napoleon Brumm was running for election. Born in Pottsville at the corner of Centre and

Minersville Streets in 1838, Brumm was one of the more colorful and controversial figures in the county. As a young man he was sent to Harrisburg along with Benjamin Bannan, the Pottsville newspaper publisher, on a mission directed by a number of leading citizens. These two gentlemen were to lobby for the passage of laws designed to create a special police force, to authorize a new criminal court having jurisdiction in Schuylkill County, and to create a new system of selecting the pool of jurors in court cases. Their supporters hoped that these progressive laws would suppress the high level of violence and disorder that was sweeping the coal region area. Because of the serious problems at this time, many people throughout the state believed that criminals charged with murder and other high crimes could not be convicted in Schuylkill County.

"If you want to get away with murder, then commit it in Schuylkill County" was a euphemism that many believed was painfully true. Brumm was one of them.

Afterwards, young Brumm completed his law studies and requested admission to the Schuylkill County Bar. Shockingly, he was refused on the grounds that his prior actions were derogatory to the character and reputation of the Schuylkill County Court system. It took him two and one half years to finally gain admission after some backroom finagling.

As for Bannan, his allegations of "lax administration of justice" resulted in his three arrests for libel. Libel suits were quite common in Pottsville in those days, giving the county barristers much business.

Brumm had been elected to Congress for a number of non-consecutive terms, and in 1906, the centennial year of Pottsville, he was running another campaign. This was his last congressional battle, but it would not, however, mark the end of his political career. To help in this campaign, Charlie Brumm had called upon the assistance of an old boyhood friend, Captain Jack Crawford, the famed Indian Scout. Jack toured on the western lecture circuit, commanding up to $100 per lecture. He was a national celebrity, but for his good friend, Charles Brumm, he spoke on his behalf at no charge. Crawford left New Mexico and headed east to Pottsville to be with his friend during his time of need.

Brumm greeted his comrade, Jack Crawford, when he alighted from the train at the Pennsylvania station. "Jack! The years have been kind to you. It's great to be back home with you, thank you for your loyalty over the years."

Watching these two individuals together presented quite a contrast. Both old men had striking personalities, with clear-cut, decisive features, bright, pleasing, all-seeing eyes. Brumm had a smooth face while his comrade wore "General Custer" long locks, a goatee, and a pronounced moustache. Crawford, the plainsman, warrior, cowboy, poet, and Indian hunter, appeared on the platform in broadcloth and a shirt, looking about at all of the changes in Pottsville. Not to be outdone, the Congressman wore his usual large hat, but with his great coat of the plains, a gift given to him by Crawford years ago.

Jack Crawford was one of the county's most unique figures, a real treasure. Born in County Donegal, Ireland, he immigrated to the United States as a very young child. Settling in Minersville, he only attended school for four days, managing to parlay this four-day education into spectacular success story.

"I don't know one rule of grammar, and I can't recite the multiplication table for the life of me," he would often tell his audience.

Despite his age of sixty-one, agile Crawford was still quite the athlete. At the Brumm reelection rally, he palmed both hands on the floor without bending his knees, and then kicked his foot higher than his head, a feat many of the young men in the audience could not do.

"The country needs Charlie Brumm, now more than ever. The reactionary forces are ready to undo the work that Teddy Roosevelt has worked so hard for."

Crawford fervently spoke in favor of the re-election of his lifelong friend, Charlie Brumm; his speech flowing with his natural wit and oratorical grace. He paid Brumm a splendid tribute as a man, a lawyer, a neighbor, and a veteran soldier. He energized his performance, probably his last one in Pottsville, with a few lariat tricks that had the audience applauding for more. One young man heckled Jack when he began speaking, with apparent reference to his long, flowing hair.

"Hey, Jack! Is your barber on strike?"

"No, young man, He is just taking a long rest" was the quick response.

Another in the crowd quipped, "Your barber will need another rest once he tackles that wig you are wearing!"

Although the crowd roared with laughter, Jack simply winked at the young, spontaneous comedian, and continued with a few more of his rope tricks. Placing the lariat down, Crawford recited several of his popular poems with each ode greeted with hearty applause.

"Let me tell you a story of my life as a young child in Schuylkill County," Crawford bellowed to the crowd as he recounted a number of touching stories from his boyhood days as well as his later life on the plains, the latter mesmerizing the audience who hung onto his every word of adventure.

Jack Crawford later announced his controversial position on alcohol. He was a firm believer in abstinence, a virtue he developed as a promise to his dear, departed mother, Suzie Wallace Crawford. His apparent physical and mental good health was attributed to abstinence from alcohol. The guest speaker, one of the first national celebrities to campaign for a political candidate, closed his performance with his temperance poem dedicated to his mother:

> "Oh, my brother, do not drink it,
> Think of all your mother said;
> While upon her death-bed laying,
> Or perhaps she is not dead;
> Don't you kill her, then, I pray you,
> She has got enough of cares,
> Sign the pledge, and God will help you,
> If you think of mother's prayers."

Captain Jack was not the only notable personality to campaign in the town on behalf of a candidate that centennial year. On September 21st, the wiry Eugene Debs, Socialist candidate for President of the United States in 1900 and 1904, arrived by train in Pottsville to campaign for the candidate of his fledgling party who was running against Brumm. The candidate was the tall and angular Cornelius Foley, one of the borough's most charismatic citizens.

Standing over six feet tall, the muscular speaker, "Con" Foley, with his long arms and a luxuriant crop of waving hair, stood out among his fellow townspeople. After moving to Pottsville from Mahanoy Plane, Foley became active as an organizer for the National Barbers' Union before devoting himself to the cause of Socialism. His deep-seated political convictions took him across the country touring as one of the Socialist Party's premier orators.

Mr. Foley was a barber by profession, living and working at 320 North Centre Street in Pottsville. Needless to say, he was a bitter opponent of Charles Napoleon Brumm. His obsession with the incumbent would continue for many years after the 1906 campaign. On this night, however, all of the attention was focused on Eugene Debs, now speaking before a full house at Union Hall, located near the Academy of Music, fielding questions posed by the progressive Attorney, William Wilhelm.

The balding Debs appeared on the stage dressed in his vest and bow tie, with his long, bony body moving about as he spoke to the crowd. The union organizer, and national politician, captivated his attentive, but polite audience, but to no avail. When the ballots were all finally counted, Brumm overwhelmingly had defeated both Foley and his Democrat opponent. The Socialists' county support was greatest in the Shenandoah area, but still a minority; Debs' fiery words did not seem to resonate with the Pottsville crowd, or with the rest of Schuylkill County in general. The Socialists found their strongest support in neighboring

Berks County, as by this time, the Reading Socialist Party organization had grown so large that it holds the balance of power in the city, and would continue to do so for the next thirty years.

> "Socialism is first of all a political movement of the working classes clearly defined and uncompromising, which aims at the overthrow of the prevailing capitalist system…Every sympathizer with labor, every friend of justice, every lover of humanity should support the Socialist party as the only party that is organized to abolish industrial slavery, the prolific source of the giant evils that afflict the people."

The determined Debs espoused these words for years to come.

Although he was victorious, Brumm soon would bring charges of ballot box fixing against several judges of election, alleging that there were more ballots in the Shenandoah boxes than votes cast. A trial was held in June of 1907 and the defendants, represented by two highly competent attorneys, Harry O. Bechtel and Adolph Schalck, were found "not guilty, but assessed the court costs." Having court costs assessed on a non-guilty party was not unusual in Schuylkill County in those days. It made the county unique in the administration of justice within the state and nation.

The Governorship was also on the line in 1906 and Pottsville was visited by probably its least liked candidate for that office, Homer Castle. Mr. Castle had the distinction of heading the Prohibition Party's ticket. You can be certain that the principles of the party were not well received in a town hosting over forty-four saloons.

> "The widely prevailing system of the licensed and legalized sale of alcoholic beverages is so ruinous to individual interests, so inimical to public welfare, so destructive of national wealth and so subversive of the rights of great masses of our citizenship, that the destruction of the traffic is, and for years has been, the most important question in American politics."

A crowd of ninety-five men and boys attended his rally at Hummel's Hall on Market Street. The fact that women had yet to receive the right to vote explains the absence of females that evening. It appeared that most of those in attendance came to hear the Third Brigade Band, which was hired by the Party. The band was a sure draw for any event, political or social. Dr. W.C. Lindenmuth introduced the candidate, and endorsed the principles of prohibitionism.

The prohibition philosophy would always remain unpopular in Pottsville and Schuylkill County, as many residents maintained a strong relationship with local breweries and saloons. Prohibitionists were about as popular in the county as atheists—no, probably less popular.

Castle was not the most prominent prohibitionist to come to Pottsville. In July 1903, the legendary activist, Carrie Nation, visited Pottsville, lecturing at Dolan's Park. For fifteen cents, or a quarter for grandstand seating, one heard the fiery orator denounce demon rum. Unfortunately for her supporters, only one hundred came to hear her that day, many of them vaulting the fence rather than pay the admission charge. Afterwards she departed to her quarters at the Tumbling Run Hotel, where she ordered whiskey at the bar and then deliberately spilled it on the floor. Despite the controversial nature of her visit and accompanying publicity, she failed to convince Pottsville to turn away from alcohol. Many a man would later regretfully look down at the Hotel floor where the precious alcohol was wasted.

In October 1906, President Theodore Roosevelt, beloved in Schuylkill County for peaceful settlement of the Great Coal Strike of 1902, visited Harrisburg for the dedication of the new state capitol building. His Pottsville supporters traveled by train to hear him speak. Many skeptics at the time referred to the new structure as "Pennsylvania's Colossal Temple of Fraud" due to its cost that was three times over budget. St. Peter's Basilica Cathedral in Rome was the inspiration for the impressive granite building and it attracted national attention in the fall of 1906. On the platform stood Senator Boise Penrose, the political boss of the state at the time. Penrose ascended to the throne of the political organization founded by Simon Cameron, strengthened by his son, James Donald Cameron, and later by Matthew Stanley Quay. Quay, who had died in 1904, was considered by most political observers to be "the boss of bosses in the United States." Author Upton Sinclair would later write the following about U.S. Senator Quay:

> "In the year 1904 there passed from his earthly reward in Pennsylvania a United States senator who had been throughout his lifetime a notorious and unblushing corruptionist...He bought the organization, bribed or intimidated the press, got his grip on the public service, including even the courts; imposed his will on Congress and Cabinet, and upon the last three Presidents—making the latter provide for the offal of his political machine, which even Pennsylvania could no longer stomach—and all without identifying his name with a single measure of public good, without making a speech or uttering a party watchword, without even pretending to be honest, but solely because, like Judas, he carried the bag and could buy whom he would."

Pursuant to the terms of the United States Senator's last will and testament, there was to be no formal inventory done of his assets. Rumors circulated wildly that his estate was worth approximately $8 million, an enormous amount of money. . At that time no inventory or appraisement was required, and there were no inheritance taxes in place; as a result, the rumors were never dispelled.

All said and done, the gilded age for politicians was in full swing.

The Republican political organization was based upon the control of patronage, the distribution of state funds among favored banks, the support of the Pennsylvania railway and other great corporations, and upon the ability of the leaders to persuade the electors that it is necessary to vote the straight Republican ticket to save the protective system. Boise Penrose, Quay's successor, immortalized for his quote, "public office is the last refuge of a scoundrel," was a big man with a big appetite. Penrose weighed over three hundred pounds and reportedly consumed a breakfast of a dozen eggs, twelve rolls, a quart of coffee and a half-inch slab of ham. However, there is no record of what he ate in Harrisburg that October morning.

The Harrisburg dedication was a splendid event, despite the heavy rain. The politicians all complimented each other for the fine work done on behalf of the citizens of the great Commonwealth. Months later, a thorough investigation revealed that five million dollars had been wasted primarily for furnishings and fixtures by corrupt officials. The fight for justice against corruption was not easy and never would be.

There would be another acrimonious election in 1907, this time for a county judgeship. Much of the local press considered Pottsville attorney, Richard Koch, to be a maverick Republican at the time. His opposition continuously chastised him for being in league with the corporate interests that desired to buy the judicial seat, and he was continuously held out as an object of scorn and ridicule. The Democrats, who controlled most of the county offices at this time, ran a strong campaign, relentlessly painting Koch as a tool of the coal companies and railroads.

In the early 1900s, Schuylkill County had six times as much coal land as the combined total of both Luzerne and Lackawanna counties to the north. Those two counties had a collective assessment of $225,000,000. Schuylkill County with its coal reserves at least six times higher had an assessment value of but $53,000,000. If the coal reserves were assessed as they had been in Luzerne and Lackawanna counties, the assessed value would have been approximately one billion fifty million dollars. These figures indicated the power of the coal companies and railroads in the county.

Koch's opponent was Harry O. Bechtel, the son of the retiring and powerful president judge. Not to be left defenseless, the Koch supporters fired highly explosive charges of their own during and after the campaign. Bechtel was accused of campaigning in saloons and buying votes in the Shenandoah area, as well as being a tool of the powerful county breweries. As supporting evidence, many pointed out that Bechtel was a director of the Union Brewing Company, located in Minersville.

The Miners Journal newspaper came out strongly for Koch and ran a series of articles on the wrongs of his father, Oliver Bechtel, the retiring President Judge. The paper basically laid the blame for the high crime rate on the substantially high number of saloon licenses granted by Judge Bechtel. The paper charged bold, brazen nepotism for the current judge of thirty years to handpick his son as his successor. Congressman Charles Napoleon Brumm jumped into the fray; he campaigned for Koch, alleging that Bechtel was a "corruptionist." Interestingly, one confidante to United States Senator Boise Penrose, the Republican boss at the time, was quoted as saying that "the election of Koch would simply have meant glorification for the reformers." The other major paper, The Pottsville Republican, which generally lived up to its name, came out squarely against the election of Koch and encouraged all of its readers to vote for his opponent. Koch was overwhelmingly defeated at the polls in that rancorous election.

1908 would also be highly politically charged year as national, state and local elections were held, with the Republicans sweeping the county, from President Taft down to the row offices. Charles Napoleon Brumm decided not to seek reelection that year, but rather seek one of the two open county judicial seats.

Victory was once again his, as he was elected to the prestigious post at the ripe old age of seventy-two, defeating his democratic opponent, Adolph Schalk, the current County solicitor. The well-bearded and well-respected Schalk had made a name for himself in the recovery of thousands of dollars for the county during the investigation of the graft scandal, which occurred during the erection of the county courthouse in the early 1890s.

Needless to say, Brumm was legendary in the county and his legend would continue to grow. The hard-of-hearing, aging Brumm would now forego the trappings of Washington, D.C. and ascend the bench of Schuylkill County.

His judicial tenure would not be a quiet one.

PART II

CHAPTER 7

▼

FIRE!

I remember having to cover a fire in the swanky section of town. As another large fire broke out in Minersville simultaneously, I covered that local blaze. That was one of the first times that I ventured into the world of Pottsville's elite. It was certainly not a normal day in the neighborhood, but I learned a lot by watching the goings on. Out on the streets I saw basically a Who's Who from the local social register, or Blue Book. I was never a wealthy person. All of my riches are found in the dog that I own. Having a dog that loves you unconditionally makes you the richest man in the world.

The fire protection in the town dated back to 1833, with the Humane Hose and Steam Fire Company. Some of these early fire departments furnished many boys who went to the front during the Civil War. Being a firefighter in Pottsville was an incredible honor. I'm sorry that I never became one.

"Fire! Sound the alarm! Quick! Sound the alarm! Fire!"

In the early morning hours of Sunday March 25, 1907, the year following the Pottsville centennial, the stable hands of Major Heber S. Thompson at Fifteenth and Mahantongo Street noticed first the smoke coming from the mansion house, followed quickly by the orange and yellow flames dancing in the dawn's early light. The palatial Cullum residence, one block away was on fire!

Immediately one stable hand yelled, "Fire!" He raced down the sidewalk and up the steps leading to the house, startling the Cullum employees who were quietly eating breakfast in the servants' kitchen. One quick thinking maid ran up the stairs to awaken the sleeping family.

"Mr. Cullum! Mrs. Cullum! Get up! Fire! Get Up! Get the children out of the burning house. Hurry!"

Another Thompson worker sounded the alarm at the corner firebox. The alarm sounded the bell whistle at the shops, as well as the bell in the tower of the town council building on Third Street. The alarm also alerted the West End Hose Company, located a few blocks away on Market Street; help was immediately needed. The volunteer firemen arrived on the scene as quickly as possible, but the muddy town streets definitely had slowed them. The men of the American Hose Company followed the West End Company. The "West Enders" had no steamer and, on coupling to the fireplug, found that their water stream had neither the force nor the quantity to fight the fire effectively. The fire fighters quickly hooked their hose to the line of the American Hose, which was connected one block away to the east. In a time of urgency, competing groups can work together for the common good.

While this was going on, the fire gained headway and the large roof of the beautiful structure was now in flames, heating up the cold March morning air. Alarms kept sounding and other fire departments kept arriving on the scene, including the Good Intent from Pottsville, The Phoenix Hook and Ladder Company and even the Good Will from Minersville, the mining community to the west of Pottsville. All of the heroic firemen discovered that they have their work cut out for them on that cold morning as they were pitted against a fire of devastating proportions, one that had the ability to not only destroy property but one that could snuff out life.

One fire chief bellowed to his men, "Our plan of attack is to try and contain the fire to the third floor of the residence. Hurry men, we don't have much time. Make sure any women and children are out of the line of danger and kept back." While the firemen bravely followed their orders and fought the flames, civilian volunteers removed the furnishings and personal effects of the Cullum family from the lower floors.

Mr. and Mrs. Cullum quickly wakened their two young children, grabbed them out of bed and hurriedly escorted them out of the house to safety. The parents were aware of the savagery of this particular fire, but they did not want to alarm the youngsters.

"The firemen will put out the fire and everything will be fine, children."

Someone, maybe a fireman or a spectator, muttered that the burning house of the wealthy owners reminded him of Schuylkill County, as he watched the upper class neighbors carrying out the exquisite personal belongings. When asked if he meant it was symbolic of the cohesiveness of the county residents, he responded negatively.

"I was referring to the great county coal wealth that was extracted by the rich and powerful from Philadelphia and New York, leaving us in ruins. I was thinking of Stephen Girard and Franklin Gowen, my boy, not these folks."

In any event, the distinguished neighbors include Ulmers, Bechtels, Zerbeys, Farquhars, Carpenters, Archibalds, Kaerchers, Shays, Rickerts, Halberstadts, Greens, and many prominent others who carried out the silverware, expensive chinaware, lamps, chandeliers, heirlooms, books, linens, hand-carved bureaus, rare artwork and other items that made the house so special. With their courageous help much was rescued, although the large lawn was littered with the clothing and furs that were damaged or destroyed by the flames.

The beautiful grand piano was carried to safety by eight men down the thirty steps that lead to Howard Avenue, and then along the street for five hundred feet, before descending twenty more steps to the Hughes home. This was one of their small victories but to the dismay of the sizable group that had gathered, the contents of the wine cellar were a total loss to the ravages of the long two-hour fire.

Large crowds often appear to watch fire departments battle the numerous blazes that torment the coal region communities. Youngsters have always been fascinated by fire and this one drew many as spectators, gawking at the splendid treasures that were carted from the disaster area. Many of the goods that escaped fiery destruction were eventually carried to the nearby home of Mr. Zerbey, the newspaper publisher. Joseph Zerbey, his wife, Cora, and their children reside at the corner mansion one block westward up the avenue. Cora Zerbey, the daughter of a Civil War Colonel, had the discipline to organize her family members and servants into marching the valuables from the fire area to the safety of her home.

"Thank you, thank you so much. May God bless each and every one of you for your brave and courageous sacrifice."

Mrs. Cullum was sincerely grateful to each and every one of the firemen and neighbors as the fire was officially declared "out." The house, intended only as a summer home, was to be occupied by the family between trips to Europe; now it is uninhabitable.

Her husband was called upon to give an impromptu interview to the various news reporters that covered the blaze.

"I was going to have the property thoroughly improved and make several improvements. I had already erected the barn and garage at the rear. The architect that was hired by me had completed his plans, but I was waiting for the warmer weather before any construction. I most likely will tear the whole house down and put up an entirely new one. My wife and I are thoroughly delighted with the locality in Pottsville, and we have decided that this is where we want our house to be."

An investigation of the cause of the fire pointed to a faulty chimney flue. Soon afterwards the West End Fire Department voted to purchase an Amoskeag steam fire engine from the International Power Company, as well as other equipment to assist in extinguishing other fires within the town. The town would be better prepared the next time, and there would always be a next time in the coal region.

CHAPTER 8

▼

HANGINGS

Prior to my entering the United States Army, I witnessed several executions in Potts-ville. It seems that during that time period these executions were regular affairs. To me, the executions were public displays drawing large crowds of citizens to witness the ultimate display of state power. I think that the public's role in the execution was to cleanse the community of the guilt and anger it harbored. They also permitted the town people to join in the condemnation of the criminal actions.

The first execution in Pottsville occurred in 1875 when young Joe Brown was hanged for the death of a married couple. There were quite a number of hangings since then. I can't recall the total number. When you think about it, John Donne, the English poet was right when he said "All our life is but a going out to the place of execution, to death."

Prior to the 1908 high school graduation, Pottsville held one of its periodic executions. That is, the town hosted a public hanging much like the hangings done over the years ever since the courthouse was relocated from Orwigsburg. This was one of the responsibilities, or benefits, depending on your point of view, placed on the town for being the county seat. The convict, young nine-teen-year-old Frank Radzius, had a scheduled appointment with the grim reaper. He had only been in Schuylkill County four months before he committed his heinous crimes, the homicide of a young mother and her four-year-old child, and he had only been in the United States four years. The weapon was a large knife and the motive appeared to be revenge over a trivial incident. The defendant barely lived to stand trial, as a crowd of several thousand in Shenandoah had gathered to lynch him. It took more than twenty-five officers to protect him from the mob. He soon stood trial, was convicted by a jury of his peers, and sentenced to death by hanging.

One versed in Greek mythology could visualize the Greek Furies stationed outside the prison doors that May, horrible to look at with their snakes for hair and blood dripping from their eyes. Yes, one could visualize the three trying to get in and keep company with Radzius. *Tisiphone*, the Avenger of Murder, *Megaera*, the Jealous One, and *Alecto* of Constant Anger.

More than five hundred citizens appeared for Radzius' May execution in the prison yard. Twelve of them were the jurors that found him guilty, unanimously voting for the death penalty. Another five hundred waited outside the prison yard, anxiously hoping that they could enter and watch the gory spectacle. The evening before the hanging, the condemned man spent several hours in prayer and meditation with local clergy. Radzius expressed his willingness to go quietly to his death. His last meal consisted of high protein portions of steak and eggs. The condemned man must have anticipated that he needed all of the strength that he could muster as he would soon climb up and onto the floor of the gallows, with the executioner waiting with noose in hand. Yes, his final performance required lots of high energy protein that morning.

At ten o'clock Radius followed behind Sheriff Evans; the long, slow procession across the prison yard to the carefully erected wooden gallows had now commenced. Dressed in his drab prison garb, Radzius walked slowly up the stairs of death, careful not to offer any final words to the curious, gawking crowd. It appeared as if this doomed man was not even aware of the crowd as he kept his eyes focused on the small silver crucifix that he held in his outreached hands. Prison physician Guldin fixed the black cap that covered his head. It would soon be over and the crowd quieted down, hoping to hear the words of both the executioner and the doomed convict.

At 10:05 Deputy Sheriff Smith gave the signal to the executioner, and with the simple hand gesture the drop fell beneath the condemned man. Immediately, you could see the body plunge downwards through the swinging doors of the trap. No sooner had the body reached the end of rope, than the physicians present for this grim task crowded about to observe the dying process close-up. Radzius was declared dead thirteen minutes later. His neck had been broken by the fall, and the noose had slipped around from beneath the left ear to the rear of the neck. The body was finally cut down, after swinging to and fro for a total of twenty-one minutes, and removed to the morgue that was part of the prison hospital.

"Justice was now served…We stand avengers at his side,
Decreeing, *Thou hast wronged the dead:*
We are doom's witnesses to thee
The price of blood his hands have shed,
We wring from him; in life, in death,
Hard at his side are we!"

—Chorus of the Furies

The Sheriff announced that the execution was one of the most successful in the history of the county. The crowd was hungry to get a souvenir and many moved towards the scaffold to get a small piece to take home. The Sheriff finally drew his pistol, firing into the air when someone in the crowd appeared to be leaning forward to grab the hangman's noose. Supposedly, getting part of the hangman's noose after an execution gave one magical powers. Superstitions were widely believed in the county at that time, by people of all nationalities.

Almost twenty-five doctors, including forty two year old Pottsville physician and coroner Alexander L. Gillars, were there on the platform. The medical practitioners conversed among themselves about the phases that a person passes through during the process they were witnessing. Other doctors in attendance included sixty-six year old William Henry Robinson, one of Pottsville's most successful practitioners as well as a civic leader, and a new young doctor, John J. Moore. The numerous doctors witnessed for themselves the death of a fellow human being as if it were a laboratory experiment. Yes, there were many doctors up on the platform at that time, a regular who's who in the local medical society. It was safe to say that Miss Swayze, the town's only female physician was not present, as no women were ever allowed to witness a hanging.

Later in that same year most of these doctors gathered together at the Panther Valley farm of colleague, Patrick O'Hara for the annual medical professional picnic. They were driven to the farm in carriages to feast upon a Pennsylvania Dutch dinner of chicken and waffles and for desert—cigars. Just what the doctor ordered! Whether the hanging they had witnessed was a topic of discussion is only speculation, but I would wager that it certainly was.

There truly was a sense of camaraderie among the physicians in those days, whether watching an execution or dining on chicken and waffles.

"There were a lot of doctors there. I didn't see young Striegel there. Was he there?" asked one gawker to his companion as they headed back towards Centre Street.

"It's difficult to say. All those doctors sort of look alike. I am not sure if Striegel had completed his studies at the University of Philadelphia yet. He sure was a bright boy and will make a fine doctor. He hopes to set up a practice here in town. He graduated from Pottsville High in 1902, along with that Brown fellow. You know, the musician. A lot of talent in the class of 1902, that's for sure."

No, John Striegel, the classmate of Robert Brown, was not present that day and he would not arrive back to town until 1910, setting up his office on East Norwegian Street.

The Radzius hanging was the second execution to occur in the town since the centennial celebration. The year before, 1907, the town hosted the hanging of Charlie Wartzel. George probably watched the hanging with the large crowd that had gathered on Lawton's Hill on the east side of town. There were many men, women and children waiting and watching, and most of them resided on that side of town.

Whether or not young George Simon was in the crowd that morning, he could not have avoided hearing or reading about the details. What lessons may a young lad learn from an experience such as a public hanging? Think about it for a moment, such a barbarous punishment.

To stand on the scaffold is an ignominious degradation. The humiliation builds slowly. First with the death sentence of a jury of one's peers, and then followed with long days of waiting on the court appeals. Then the condemned man has his last night in his cell covered by the hungry newspaper reporters. What does the condemned man have for his last meal on earth? How much time does he spend with the clergy who are worried over his soul being thrown into eternal damnation. Then there is the long, slow walk to the scaffold. Will there be final words given, or not? The executioner then places the black cap over the head and quickly the noose is drawn tight around the neck that will soon be broken by the state. The crowd gawks, anxiously trying to get a better look as the body sways slowly back and forth like a pendulum.

George Simon would not in a thousand years ever allow himself to be placed in such a situation. He was a good, boy who learned the difference between right and wrong at a young age. He firmly believed in God and said his prayers, an active member of his Lutheran congregation. Yet, he was a romantic who certainly enjoyed material possessions, needing handsome, stylish clothing and spending money to ensure that Viola would remain with him forever. His faith would not stand in his way and neither would his parents. In any event, George would never let himself get into such a predicament such as Radzius or Wartzel. He would never allow himself to go to prison. From what he had heard, the place was filled with lice, roaches, degenerates and bedbugs. Utterly disgusting.

"I will never, ever allow myself to be taken up the scaffold," thought the Simon lad, knowing that he was already on a path to destruction.

He had wanted fancy dress shirts, silk hats, and pocket watches. His mother longed to have the house painted and wallpapered, especially the spare bedroom.

George was completely self-centered, thinking only of himself. In Greek mythology, Narcissus was a handsome young man destroyed due to his self-absorption. Today psychologists, to describe an emotionally immature person, use the term "narcissist." Later many would give that label to George.

What was more important, fixing up the house, or enjoying his senior year at Pottsville High? The answer was easy to the selfish son. My God, his parents had given in to his every desire. Whatever he set his fancy on, his parents made sure he received. Yet, he could not have enough. He always wanted more. Greed was considered one of the seven deadly sins and this vice now captured George Simon's free will. He would never have enough money and when he obtained some, he spent it willfully on anything that he desired. Sometimes his conscience bothered him and he would spend some of his ill-gotten gains on charities and on others. That was when the "good" George took control of him. It did not happen often. The money that he spent certainly was impressive to his Pottsville High classmates, who wondered where his good fortune came from. Whenever asked about the money, George would simply tell them that he the funds came from a very wealthy uncle that loved him dearly.

CHAPTER 9

▼

HIGH SCHOOL

Here are school year books from years ago. I marked the pictures of some of the students. Look, here are the pictures of George Simon and Viola, as well as the photographs of Joel Boone and his sweetheart, Helen Koch.

Did you ever see that movie, "Angels with Dirty Faces?" The two youths in the film are Jimmy Cagney, who has the role of Rocky Sullivan, and Pat O'Brien as his best friend Jerry. Rocky became a swaggering, pugnacious criminal, while his best friend, Jerry became a priest. Two children from the same environment turn to entirely different lifestyles. George and Joel came from the same area and sang together in the glee club. They remind me of Rocky and Jerry.

Isn't it strange how people in similar situations can take such different future paths?

Pottsville High School was located at the corner of Fifth and Norwegian Streets in the center of Pottsville; the building was named after the slain president James Garfield along with the town square. The large beautiful, stone Romanesque Revival style, fortress of education was erected in 1893. The entire third floor was used for the high school. High school consisted of a three-year program until 1912 when it added the extra year that continues to this day. For the young Simon boy, the high school was ideally located within six blocks from the home of the most beautiful girl in the City of Pottsville. Viola.

At the time of the centennial, Professor Stephen Thurlow, a graduate of Amhurst College in Massachusetts, served as the high school principal. The Professor was a noted intellectual, and his curriculum was very demanding for his students. All the same, he was well revered, and in 1906, after the death of Reverend Patterson, he was appointed the school district superintendent. His successor was the equally demanding Professor Joseph Kehler, who had a striking physical resemblance to John Wilkes Booth. Both professors insisted on excellence from their students. The curriculum of high school required that the first year students study History, Algebra, Geometry, Latin, Caesar, and Elocution. The middle year courses consisted of Physiology, Literature, Botany, Composition, Cicero, Latin Prose, Caesar, Elocution, and Physical Geography. The senior year courses were Physics, Cicero, Virgil, Rhetoric, Civics, Astronomy, Trigonometry, Chemistry, Geology and Elocution. As I said, the school's curriculum challenged the students.

George Simon participated in the numerous activities that the school offered. The nineteen-year-old, blue-eyed, blonde-haired senior even played on the school's football team, but he certainly was not one of its stars. He weighed 140 pounds and measured five feet and nine inches tall. That was about average for a player in those days. In fact, the heaviest player on the team was his teammate Wessinger, who weighed in at 150 pounds. Nutrition professionals have records that indicate that the average nineteen year old male weighed 133 pounds in the 1890s, 139 pounds in the 1900s, 156 pounds in the 1920s and 160 pounds in the 1930s; as you can see, a steady progression with the average weight increasing over time. Most likely, George Simon would be considered underweight, or puny, if he tried out for the team today.

Other activities that attracted young Simon's attention included the debating club, Phi Epsilon Kappa, as well as its Glee Club. This school singing club had been reorganized under the tutelage of Robert Brown, a graduate of the class of 1902, and the young man considered a musical genius. Now known as Braun, his energy and innate talent to generate beautiful music seemed unlimited. Returning to Pottsville, he earned an appointment as the organist and choirmaster of Trinity Episcopal Church on Centre Street leading a boys' choir of sixty-five. He was also attracting many students to his private music academy.

The Pottsville High Glee Club was an all male singing group, with all of the boys performing in handsome tuxedos and ties. While singing in the club as a baritone, George could forget his wickedness and focus his energy on the music. He rarely missed the glee club practices that were held in preparation for the extravaganza—the yearly concert at the High School Assembly Room. "Comin

Thro' the Rye" and "The Wind is Blowing High, Love" were two of the songs
that he would sing repeatedly in anticipation of impressing both his parents and
his beloved, Viola.

One of his schoolmates, and a fellow Glee Club member, was Joel Boone, a
year or two his junior. While George lived with two loving parents who devoted
everything to their son, Joel's background was quite different. His father was
oppressive and young Joel could recollect little about his mother. In fact, when
asked, he would state that his last remembrance of his mother was watching her
wave good-bye to him as she journeyed off to Philadelphia. Her destination was
the far away hospital where she underwent surgery for her cervical cancer. Unfortunately, she died shortly after the operation. The motherless child now remained
with his strict father who conducted a hay and grain business in St. Clair.

Young Joel assisted with all of the drudgery associated with stable work. If he
did not do as he was told, old Mr. Boone became physically abusive, especially
after drinking heavily. After his father's remarriage, young Joel was forced to
adjust to life with both a stepmother and the stepmother's mean-spirited daughter.

"Joel," asked his stepmother, "I think you'd be better off moving away from
your father. You should go away to a school where you could devote all of your
time to your studies. You will make a fine doctor, if only you get the time necessary. I have some information on the Mercersburg Academy. It is a fine school,
and I know you will be happy there."

The young man's redemption was achieved by taking his stepmother's advice
to transfer from Pottsville High School and live away from home. Although, he
was unsure if he wanted to leave his friends, he had a burning ambition to pursue
a career in medicine. His stepmother promised him that the change would be for
the better. He left Schuylkill County after his middle year at Pottsville High
School, graduating from Mercersburg Academy in 1909, the year after George
Simon graduated from Pottsville.

Joel would soon leave Pottsville High, its glee club and track team. After
receiving his diploma from the Academy he enrolled at Hahnemann Medical
School in Philadelphia, soon after joining the Navy and marrying his home town
love, Helen Koch, the daughter of the recently defeated judicial candidate, Richard Henry Koch.

Helen Koch was truly Joel Boone's childhood sweetheart. They first met when
he was ten years old after she arrived at one of his sister's birthday parties. His
brunette sweetheart was not only attractive, she was a determined and intelligent
student, an accomplished pianist and popular with her classmates. The two were

inseparable, spending what free time that they had at Tumbling Run where they could picnic, dance, swim, and boat, and plan for their future together as husband and wife.

For a time however, Joel Boone was on the stage, singing his heart out with fellow glee club members, George Simon among them, to the tune *"Comin Thro' the Rye."* Little did anyone imagine what different paths lay ahead for those two high school boys, both dressed in their spotless tuxedos, white shirts and black ties, as they continued their melodic verses under the watchful eye of family members and friends.

George Simon, without doubt, would make something of himself someday, his parents were certain. To them he was intelligent, good looking, strong and athletic, with a good singing voice to boot. Yet, they were puzzled why George did not have close friends. He had several acquaintances but no real male friends. It appeared as if the other students did not want to associate with him. Mr. and Mrs. Simons assumed that his spending too much of his time courting that girl from Norwegian Street may be the answer. George could be successful, if he would only put his mind to it, and keep his faith in God.

His parents were pleased that George was taking an interest in church work. As so many others would, he often recited the Lord's Prayer with its plea for spiritual assistance in the words first spoken by Jesus Christ.

"Lead us not into temptation, but deliver us from evil."

Yes, George believed that a person needed divine guidance to gain control of the darker side of human nature, and to stop the seed of evil from growing larger and taking full control. To receive this spiritual guidance, he became an active member of Trinity Reformed Lutheran, a popular church with about 1200 members, located just below Garfield Square. The congregation had been created when local Lutherans acted on a desire for liturgy to be spoken in the English language, rather than German. The church's new pastor had just been installed in August 1907, Reverend A.J. Reiter, who came from New Wales. Pastor Reiter was well received by his parishioners and the community in general; he made friends quickly, and one of his best friends would be band director Fred Gerhard.

The Pottsville High School graduation in 1908 was expected to be a time for celebration for Mr. and Mrs. Simon, as they had saved their meager funds to send their son to Drexel Institute in Philadelphia. Mr. Simon worked hard in the Delano machine shop and his life revolved around his son's future being better than his own. Work at the shop was getting scarce and old George was lucky to keep his job. Hard to comprehend that, while the very design of the locomotive engine originated in the Delano shops back in the period from 1864 to 1867, but by 1898, the economy was changing and not all changes were positive. Delano's importance was diminished when the company shifted the building of the loco-motives to Weatherly. Delano's days as an employment magnet drew to a close. Old George prayed that his job would be secured long enough to fulfill the plans that he and his wife had for their son—George would become an engineer. They envisaged him having an office job, wearing one of his fancy suits and hats. He had so many of them. Yes, George could become a professional if he set his mind to it. Someday he may even become a member of the elite Outdoor Club. He would become so successful that he could assist his parents in their old age, as they had no retirement savings to speak of.

But young George had plans other than college. College would mean being separated from Viola. He wanted to marry her when he was just a junior in high school. His love for her never diminished, despite his parents' disapproval.

"You are much too young to get married! You will go to college and meet an educated woman! It is just puppy love, George! You could never support a wife! I forbid you to see her anymore!"

George would simply ignore his mother's commands and threats.

"Why can't they understand us? We are not too young to get married, and we have been keeping company for years now?"

High School graduation was a joyous, newsworthy event in those days. It would make the front-page headlines of both the Pottsville Republican and the Miners' Journal. Before Professor Thurow distributed the diplomas, there would be the traditional Circus Day in Pottsville. The School Board announced a half-day schedule due to the high absenteeism predicted. Who wants to be in school when Buffalo Bill was coming to town to entertain the residents? Dolan's Park at 18th Street, now part of Pottsville, was the scheduled site for one of the town's favorite events—"Buffalo Bill's Wild West Show."

The sixty-two year old William Cody performed "The Battle of Summit Springs" for the large local crowd in late June. The act was one of his latest stan-dard features, based on actual events that he was personally involved in. The bat-tle took place in 1869, in retaliation for an attack by Cheyenne Indians on settlers along the Solomon River in Nebraska. Buffalo Bill led the Fifth U.S. Cavalry to the camp of Cheyenne leader Tall Bull, and allegedly dispatched the chief person-ally. This kind of exploit lent itself to spectacle in Cody's traveling show business performances. Most of the graduating class of 1908 was in attendance, watching the aging western hero give a rollicking good performance. It would be one of the last times that the classmates would spend together.

Pottsville had recently absorbed the town of Yorkville, and the now larger Pottsville was increasing in population. Not many more circuses would be held at Dolan's Park, as land there was needed for homes. Dolan's Park was prime flat land and subdivision would soon make lots available to the burgeoning middle-class.

The graduates received their diplomas during a dignified ceremony held at the Academy of Music. The confident students marched into the auditorium, the girls all dressed in white and the boys dressed in dark jackets and light trousers, with many of the notable students given seats up front with the adult dignitaries. There was Marion Sterner, the class president, Chapin Carpenter, Nesbit Frost, Elsie Hess, Ray Wadlinger and George Wood among others. Awards were handed out to Marshall Koch, for high achievement in Mathematics, and to Ray Wadlinger for high achievement in Latin. Ray was the son of the late George Wadlinger, who died at the young age of forty-three, shortly after attaining the position of county judge; leaving his widow to raise Ray and several other children. Ray was another member of the school Glee Club, and Ray loved to sing. In fact, his tenor voice would boom lyrically through the hall that graduation day. George Wood, the class orator, gave a short speech and some young woman recited the class poem, which included the cryptic words:

"So the fallen phantoms flee,
and the sharp reality now must now act its past."

Strange words recited at the graduation. Was anyone listening attentively? What did those words mean to those who were paying attention? Apparently, no one seemed to think about them much that day.

Mr. and Mrs. Simon attended the event, along with all of the other proud parents. They sat through the prayers of Father Diller, pastor of the Trinity Episcopal Church, as well as the principal's speech, before a few words were mentioned for the recently departed former President Grover Cleveland. Marshall Koch entertained with a violin solo. Anna Wilhelm, the daughter of Attorney William Wilhelm gave another speech. Sadie Golden, the class historian, supposedly gave away the class secrets. But no one could have known the secrets that lie within George Simon. They remained a secret for many more months.

His secrets would have repulsed every God-fearing person present.

The parents present on that June day were so proud. To receive a high school diploma was such an honor, as many of these parents had never had the opportunity to receive one, many being immigrants to this country. They hoped that the life of their child would be better than their own. That is almost a universal longing that transcends time and place. After the ceremony, the celebrations continued at parties throughout the town.

Music was heard at those graduation parties with many of the latest songs being played. Groups of young people gathered around a piano and sang along to the snappy new tunes of the day. One of which was "Take Me Out to the Ballgame." Everyone seemed to enjoy that one. Whenever that song was sung, the name of Jack Picus came up. Everyone was rooting for his success on the baseball diamond. That song, incidentally, was destined to be the third most popular song in the nation in several decades, right behind the national anthem and "Happy Birthday."

At graduation time in 1908 all thoughts of the joyful celebrants were on the present, with no concern of the days past or days to come. It was Abraham Lincoln who said that the best thing about the future was that it came just one day at a time, and pursuant to this Presidential decree, they sang the chorus through late in the evening.

> "Take me out to the ball game,
> Take me out with the crowd
> Buy me some peanuts and Cracker Jack,
> I don't care if I never get back.
> Let me root, root, root for the home team,
> If they don't win, it's a shame.
> For it's one, two, three strikes, you're out,
> At the old ball game."

CHAPTER 10

▼

ABOUT TOWN

You don't mind if I tell you more about Pottsville before I continue with the Simon story? I don't have many photographs of the town to share with you, but I do have several postcards. Here look at them. Look as I tell you about them. Most are of the Courthouse, the prison and the Clay Monument. Postcards are kind, as when you look at them over the years, they remain constant without change, that's more than you can say about looking at people.

Phoebe Simon and her son George walked to the downtown one crisp March Saturday morning. George was to get a haircut while his mother did some shopping. The barbershop of Cornelius Foley would fill up quickly with men waiting to get a haircut or shave, while at the same time listening to the opinionated barber espouse his views on every possible subject.

When Simon arrived two men were already waiting while Foley lathered up the face of the customer slouched in the leather seat. He was new in the area and had asked Foley to tell him about Pottsville and the county. Little did he know that this innocuous question would trigger an emotional response from the haircutter.

"Coal had been, and still is, the unrivaled king in this southern anthracite region. J. Pierpont Morgan, the financial giant, has control of the nation's railways, and the railways owned most of the coalfields. This anthracite region is therefore a de facto colony of the corporate owners that lived in New York and

Philadelphia, with most of the region's wealth flowing out to those east coast cities," Foley proclaimed with his Irish complexion turning a reddish color. "Philadelphia & Reading Coal & Iron Company owns more than 100,000 acres of coal reserves, an amount of land equal to 156.2 square miles."

While the young Simon was waiting his turn, Phoebe Simon made her way towards the Centre Street stores that offered a dazzling array of merchandise. Miehle's Department Store, located at the southwest corner of Norwegian Street, Mortimer's Hats, and Green's Jewelry Store were just a sampling of a few of the many fine stores that attracted the attention of the astute shopper. The storeowners were not only merchants; they were friends. For instance, old Mr. Mortimer operated his haberdashery at the corner of Norwegian Street. The successful merchant had studied the hatter trade for several years before opening his small store in 1864. Business was so good that, over time, the store expanded due to the demand for hats by men, women and children alike. Mr. Mortimer was aware that his customers demanded the latest in fashions and he brought to the area the finest in wearing apparel from New York City. It is astonishing that at one time he managed the store alone, before gradually adding twenty-five employees. Hats were not the only attraction in his establishment. Most of the young girls in town enjoyed entering Mortimer's "Victorian doll basement." In that special section of the store, they were treated to the one of the handsomest display of dolls anywhere in the county. The store owner was indeed one of the most popular people in the town during its centennial celebration, and this popularity continued through his blood-line as his namesake, F. Pierce, Jr. would take over the business, and also play a prominent role in the future of Pottsville.

In 1907 consumers clamored for indoor toilets and bathtubs, toasters, portable cameras, and, of course, the "Victrola." The latter was an acoustic phonograph with the sound-reproducing horn built-in to the cabinet. While the earliest phonographs used large external horns to amplify the sound, it was the invention of the internal horn Victrola in 1906 that literally launched the phonograph into millions of homes. No longer was the phonograph a strange machine with a huge horn that stood out so awkwardly in a room; the new Victrola looked like a piece of furniture that fit perfectly in the parlor; a stylish piece of furniture and an accepted item in one's parlor. "Victrola" was the brand name, and not a generic term for all old wind-up phonographs. It seemed as if every household wanted to have one in their parlor. By 1914, over one half million were sold with Pottsville having its fair share. People were able to listen to the classics as well as the popular Tin Pan Alley songs of the day from the comfort of their own homes without having to go to concert halls.

Phoebe Simon would marvel at all of the latest goods for sale, and say to herself, "Technology is wonderful isn't it?"

Fashions were also changing in this new century; instead of wearing homemade clothes, the average person now was able to have "store bought" outfits. Women were shopping in the many stores for a variety of beautiful clothes that generally consisted of floor length skirts. The ladies were wearing these outfits even when bicycling or gardening. Jewish tailors, newly arrived from Europe, and their female machine operators placed these mass-produced outfits on the market. The Sears, Roebuck Department store catalogue was now featuring one hundred and fifty versions of the latest fashion—the shirtwaist, a blouse meant to be worn with a skirt, and quite popular in Pottsville. A peek-a-boo version even allowed the flesh of a woman's arms to be visible—quite daring for its day. At about the same time "ladies walking skirts" were advertised baring a woman's ankle. "Scandalous" some old-timers said, while the younger women seemed to welcome these innovations.

Other women's apparel included the high, buttoned shoes, whalebone corsets, and hats with festive plumage and decorations. The same Sears catalogue devoted one full page to seventy-five variations of ostrich feathered hats. The men's woolen suits were almost always dark and heavy. In the summer, out in the country a man might wear white flannel, but there was no such thing as a "summer weight suit". The shirts had high collars and detachable cuffs for easier washing, but they were still warm. The 1900s were a great decade to shop for clothing, and Pottsville offered the widest selection between Philadelphia and Pittsburgh. The economy would only get better according to all prognostications.

Back at the barbershop, a youngster who walked in with his father asked aloud, "Papa, who is that a statue of staring down at the town?"

"Son, that is the famous statesman, Henry Clay. You will learn more about him in school."

Foley, who was a fount of information, placed himself within the private conversation between father and son.

"Yes, the large statue of Henry Clay hovered over the south side of the town. This monument pays tribute to United States Senator Henry Clay, of Ashland. This Ashland is not the Ashland eighteen miles north of Pottsville; it is the Ashland in Kentucky."

The child's curiosity was now aroused and he retorted. "Did Mr. Clay live in Pottsville? Was he a chief burgess?"

Yes, the inquisitive questions of a child sometimes makes an adult realize that so much has been forgotten or taken for granted, as well as remembering the world of childhood itself, so full of innocence, wonder and astonishment.

Foley responded, "When Henry Clay, the American Statesman and four time presidential candidate, died in 1852, the citizens of Pottsville, led by newspaper publisher Benjamin Bannan, decided to honor the great American Senator with a tall iron monument, completed within three years. John Bannan, a cousin to the publisher, donated the land on which the monument still stands today. Quite a feat erecting such a monument high atop that steep hill!"

"Mr. Barber, tell me more about this statue of Clay, will you please? Please Mr. Barber!"

"On a sunny June afternoon in 1855 all was ready, and John Temple, with twelve mules, succeeded in slowly pulling the statue up South Second Street followed by a large crowd of onlookers. Waters Chilson, of Palo Alto, builder of the monument, with the assistance of six men, raised the statue in one hour and fifty minutes and placed it on its tall base. The statue, at first, faced east towards Greenwood Hill and Port Carbon, but the following day the committee had it turned so that it looked north over Centre Street and Pottsville's bustling downtown. The formal dedication occurred on the following Independence Day. Young boys, a little older than you, thought that the statue was erected to honor Henry Clay for his gambling prowess. In 1829 there was a game, attributed to this public figure, being played on a steamboat bound for New Orleans, in which each player received five cards and made bets—then whoever held the highest combination of cards won all bets. He was the inventor of the card game Poker that you will play when you get older."

Another patron waiting in a wooden chair, placed his paper down and joined in, "I never heard that Clay invented the game of Poker or was a gambler."

"There are a lot of things that we don't know about our so-called government leaders. Why, Clay's gambling was legendary and the source of many a good story. His wife was once asked if she minded her husband's habitual gambling. Lucretia Clay, his wife, had grown accustomed to her husband's whiskey, cigars, womanizing, and profanities and her quick response to the question was an innocent 'Oh! Dear, no! Mr. Clay almost always wins.'"

The barber then gave a wink to the young lad, "Pottsville is a town filled with gambling halls, so it was only fitting to memorialize the inventor of poker with such a fine statue."

"Say Foley, if you know so much about Pottsville, tell us about the prison," quipped another patron.

"Philadelphia designer Napoleon LeBrun constructed the prison in 1851. LeBrun was noted for his design of many Philadelphia churches, including the monumental Cathedral of SS. Peter and Paul on Logan Square. His other major contribution to Philadelphia architecture was the Academy of Music on Broad Street. The Schuylkill County prison to this day reminds me of the French Bastille, except that there is no guillotine, only the hangman's noose. And don't get me started on that travesty of justice that occurred in 1877, when six of my native countrymen were hanged by the neck, labeled Molly Maguires, and then laid to rest."

"Papa, is that where they send bad men?" the youngster chimed.

"Yes, son. If you are real bad, you are sent there to repent for your bad actions." "I'll never go there, papa. I'm a good boy."

"Foley, now tell us about the Courthouse," asked the same questioning patron, referring to the breathtaking Pottsville courthouse with its large clock tower.

"During the second term of President Judge Cyrus L. Pershing, who presided over the travesty referred to as the Molly Maguire trials, it became necessary, due to the growth of the county, that a new courthouse be erected. This new building was built right along side the old courthouse and across the street from the old Welsh Baptist Cemetery, where some of the remains of the earliest settlers are buried"

"Foley, Judge Pershing was a well-respected jurist who was nominated for Governor in 1875 by the Democratic State convention."

"Yes, and luckily he was soundly defeated. The Courthouse was dedicated and opened for the administration of so-called justice in September 1891, at a cost of about $320,000, almost $180,000 over the initial estimate. That is not unusual in Pennsylvania as there are so many hands out."

At this time, Foley finished shaving his patron who sat silently during the conversation, probably afraid to upset the barber who had the razor over his neck.

Another man sat down in the barber chair and requested his usual haircut while another patron asked about the conditions of the working class in Pottsville.

"Tis funny that you should ask, as Dr. Halberstadt, a prominent town physician issued a dire warning immediately prior to the 1906 Centennial. He warned of the serious possibility of a typhoid epidemic. He wanted the Board of Health to take immediate precautions to protect the health and safety of the citizenry. These conditions stem from the unsanitary conditions in some of the local working class neighborhoods. The government does not do enough, and only a good solid Socialist government would take the necessary action."

"Yea, Foley. I remember that problem over in Fishbach, it had to do with the contaminated well water. There were five houses with seventy-five occupants. I wouldn't call them families. Fifty-eight or so were boarders. One widow had sixteen boarders crammed into her house."

"Foreigners they were. They were so numerous that they were compelled to sleep in the celler or on the rooftops. I heard that the stench was unbearable."

Foley continued, "As a result of the Halberstadt warnin and the news coverage that followed, the Board of Health was forced to take action to protect the citizenry from the dreaded typhoid. We need more men like Halberstadt. Tis not the fault of the so-called foreigners, as they are exploited workers just like the rest of us. The working class must begin to act together and take this country back."

The father of the inquisitive child then asked his own question to the apparent all-knowing barber, "I understand that Pottsville is letting in the Negroes. Is that true?' Foley responded affirmatively, "Tis true there are Negroes in Pottsville. Exploited workers come in all colors, shapes and shades, me lad. They are settlin mainly in our fifth ward. Many call it the 'Bloody Fifth Ward' due to the roughness and rowdiness found there. There just is not enough good housing for the working class. All workers are me friends regardless of color. I cud stand her fur another hour and tell you all about the working class."

Finishing the haircut, and brushing off the patron, George Simon now got up and made his way to the barber chair. He looked at his watch to make sure that he would be on time to walk his mother back home and carry any bundles that she may have with her.

C H A P T E R   11

▼

HEROES

Where did I get wounded? Well, it was at the second battle of the Marne in July 1918. I was an eager doughboy back then. I hurt my left leg but I walked fairly well with the assistance of a cane for several years. I am an old man now and seek the comfort of a comfortable chair. Just being old should allow me the chair without any questions being asked. You came for information on the early days of Pottsville, so let me continue.

Hell, I am no hero just because I got wounded in the war. I was just doing my job and was at the wrong place at the wrong time. But if you want to know about Pottsville's heroes, then I will digress a bit and weave the city's magnificent military history into my story.

On the busy corner at Centre and Market Street, a six-story office building was being erected, referred to as the Thompson building, in honor of its owner, Lewis C. Thompson, a hardware store merchant. The large structure would feature Otis elevators to take one up from the ground to the sixth floor. Structures such as these was making Pottsville a city rather than a typical coal town. Besides the stores that lured the crowd downtown, entertainment was also a major attraction. The Academy of Music offered the finest in concerts and stage productions, and later on, the much smaller and less ornate Majestic Theatre, opening in 1910, featured vaudeville as well as the "moving pictures" that captivated the imagination of the entire nation. The Hippodrome followed in 1913, with more seating for the ever-popular vaudeville shows.

As mentioned before, Tumbling Run was the premier location for outdoors recreation, located just a short trolley ride south of the city. It was there that the grand Tumbling Run Hotel was located. This elegant mountain resort featured an arcade with slot machines, a movie room devoted to old western motion pictures, a basketball court, a large dance area, a roller skating rink, and 65 boathouses. Its theatre showcased vaudeville at its best; one could watch monkey acts, acrobats, Hebrew singers, "all white dancing belles," and jugglers all for only ten cents or less. Some shows were even free, such as "Watson's Farmyard Circus" that featured creative chickens and ducks. Tumbling Run was also the ideal location for swimming, picnicking, and boating. Although the main tourist season ran from Decoration Day in late May until Labor Day, the locals ice-skated on the frozen waters during the winter months. Every season had something to offer at Tumbling Run and it was the trolley car that brought the large crowds.

In 1909 the automobile was still a convenience for the wealthy, and cars were not yet numerous in the county. In fact, there were only about 8,000 automobiles in the whole nation at the turn of the century. The automobile explosion, however, would soon begin in earnest with Henry Ford's revolutionary assembly line production of his Model T. Pottsville was preparing for the rising popularity of these horseless carriages.

Historians will tell you that the first gas-powered automobile purchased for commercial use made its debut in Pottsville in 1898, when one vehicle was unloaded at the Reading Station. Slowly more and more automobiles will travel on the roads throughout the county, requiring major improvements in the road surfaces in the expanded Pottsville.

The town took its first steps to abandon the cobblestone streets during the 1890s, a slow and expensive endeavor. Centre Street was first paved with Belgian granite blocks, with Metropolitan red bricks being placed on some of the other major streets. Youngsters enjoyed the paving as it provided them with the opportunity to play "kick the wicket" with the wooden blocks left by the contractors.

Market Street and the Garfield Square area also underwent paving to the relief of the populace, especially those who longed to drive a horseless carriage. The wooden blocks used on these streets were considered noiseless. Some question arose as to whether or not it would be safe for the horses to travel, but the blocks used had grooves in them, permitting horses to get a firm hold and not slip. When Market Street is finally completed, over 12,868 square yards of block will have been laid. Over one half million blocks will have been put down, all treated with a chemical for preservation to make them last for many years to come.

In February 1907, Yorkville, the forty-two year old borough adjoining Pottsville on the west, was annexed by a majority vote of the residents of both municipalities. The vote was not overwhelming as the possibility of increased taxes led many to vote against the proposal in both municipalities, each suspicious of the other. With the victory at the ballot box, Pottsville's boundaries no longer stopped at Sixteenth Street, but now extended another mile or so westward. Pottsville's future looked brighter than ever. There was a call for annexation of other smaller municipalities that bordered Pottsville, such as Palo Alto, Mount Carbon, Mechanicsville, St. Clair and Port Carbon, but the entrenched political powers in those miniscule towns would never permit what had happened to Yorkville happen to them. The Pottsville Republican newspaper editor envisioned a population of at least 50,000 if annexation of its neighbors could occur. As time went by Pottsville's boundaries would never grow again and its population, although increasing in the short run, would then peak at the mid twenty thousand range and slowly shrink.

Later that year, in July, the town was saddened by the death of Admiral Norman von Heidreich Farquhar, the brother of local attorney Guy Farquhar. Young Joel Boone, as well as all the other school children, read of the exploits of Admiral Farquhar and the Admiral's exploits certainly must have been of some inspiration.

A local boy becoming an admiral in the Unites States Navy, what a dream come true.

School was closed for the summer when the Admiral died, but young boys hungered for information concerning such a local adventurer. Farquhar had quite a biography and made a positive role model for the youth of the community.

Norman Farquhar was born in town in 1840, and quickly made himself quite a name, having attended the U.S. Naval Academy during the late 1850's. After graduation, he served with the Africa Squadron until September 1861 suppressing the slave trade, and he became a Midshipman and Acting Master from 1859–61. One of his most famous exploits that captivated the imagination of many a young boy in his hometown, was his bringing to the United States shores the captured slave ship, the *Triton*, with a crew of ten men. What made this more courageous was the fact that no other officer assisted him.

Then as a Lieutenant, he spent most of the Civil War off the U.S. Atlantic coast and in the West Indies, serving in the gunboats *Mystic*, *Sonoma* and *Mahaska* and the cruisers *Rhode Island* and *Santiago de Cuba*. Many said that the citizenry of Pottsville would forever remember the courageous exploits of Admiral Farquhar, and many a schoolboy envisioned himself taking to the high seas. However, Admiral Farquhar would be forgotten over time replaced by newer heroes and local politicians attempting to claim their own lasting legacy. Nothing in town would be named in the Admiral's honor.

Yes, Pottsville was home to many a military hero. One other was quite interesting and his story needs to be repeated, as he too was quickly forgotten. Francis M. Wynkoop, born in 1820 and was one of the nation's most distinguished soldiers. He marched with General Scott all the way from Vera Cruz to Mexico City, during the war with our southern neighbor. His military importance cannot be understated, and he was promoted to Brigadier General, outranking both Generals Ulysses S. Grant and Robert E. Lee in Mexico.

His brother, John Estill Wynkoop another famed military officer, was the owner of the large mansion house situated on Howard Avenue. Flames engulfed this house years later in March 1907, when Mr. and Mrs. J. Barlow Cullum owned it.

Isn't it interesting how persons and events in Pottsville all appear to be connected?

Unfortunately Francis Wynkoop lost his life, tragically in a hunting accident on December 13, 1857 when an assistant accidentally shot him and he bled to death. His wake was held at the residence of his brother-in-law, Thomas Atwood in Pottsville, and his remains buried on December 16th, 1857, ten years after the Mexican War. The deceased had been an editor of the Miner's Journal and later established the Anthracite Gazette. Under President Franklin Pierce he was appointed as Marshall of the Eastern District of Pennsylvania.

The Wynkoop military funeral was perhaps the largest ever held in Pottsville and perhaps the whole county. There were nineteen companies in line, along with the Scott Legion of Philadelphia. All of his Mexican War companies were mustered, plus several companies from Tamaqua and Mexican War veterans from miscellaneous outfits.

As the funeral left Trinity Episcopal Church on South Centre Street, people crowded onto the site of the Henry Clay Monument perched above the town. From that place they had an elevated view of the procession, which proceeded to Mauch Chunk Street, countermarched and proceeded to Mt. Laurel Cemetery, now renamed the Charles Baber Cemetery.

Death would not keep Wynkoop from the public eye, nor keep him from controversy. His widow assented to the burial in Pottsville at first, but later planned to have his remains removed to Philadelphia after the pageantry in town subsided. She was not as fond of Pottsville as was her husband. The mother of the deceased military officer had other plans. She had loved Pottsville dearly and her son, a Pottsville war hero, would remain there perpetually. Word was given to the cemetery wardens to forbid any trespass upon her son's gravesite. The widow and her mother-in-law then became tangled in legal proceedings that ended up in the state Supreme Court. Wynkoop's body still remains in Baber Cemetery to this day thanks to the unanimous decision of the highest court in the state handed down five years after his death.

There is absolutely no truth to the rumor that the epithet on his tombstone reads, "*I'd rather be in Philadelphia.*"

CHAPTER 12

▼

THE CLOUD HOME

Who were the wealthiest and the most powerful people living in Pottsville during this period? That is a good question. The government did not keep statistics as it does now a day. Someone told me that the richest woman in the United States today is worth about $100 million. Her name is Hetty Green Wilks. I don't know much about her. As for Pottsville, in my opinion, the two that come to mind are Charlemagne Tower, Jr. and George Baer. There will never be two people like that around the town again. They were two in two million! Let me tell you about their last meeting together along the streets of Pottsville when they had a coffee klatch with Miss Bannan, who was quiet wealthy in her own right but certainly not in the same league as Hetty Green Wilks. All my riches can be found in my dog, I think I already told you that. Unconditional love, that's what I get from that dog of mine.

Charlemagne Tower, Jr. had missed the centennial celebration, and was anxious to return to his old hometown of Pottsville the following March, even if only for a few days. His official title at the time was Ambassador Extraordinary and Plenipotentiary to Germany. The honored appointment by President Theodore Roosevelt commenced in 1902 and would last until 1908. His father, as a young patent lawyer, came to Schuylkill County to appraise coal lands in Porter Township, at the west end of the county, as well as to acquire other coal properties. Old Tower had a contingency fee arrangement with his client, Alfred Munson that he would get one half of any profit Munson would make. And profits did he make.

The young lawyer first settled in the then county seat of Orwigsburg in 1846, marrying a local girl. Two years later the couple had a son, the future Ambassador, Charlemagne, Jr. In 1853, the family moved to Pottsville, which had since become the new county seat, living for the next 24 years on Mahantongo Street. Old Charlemagne successfully entered the political world of Schuylkill County winning an election as District Attorney before joining the Union Army, rising to the rank of Captain.

Charlemagne, Sr. was a brilliant businessman, leasing 1,500 acres of the Porter Township land to independent companies who later built the Brookside and Tower collieries. With his new partner, Samuel Munson, son of his former client, Alfred Munson, Tower began to develop a small town near the collieries, which was and still is named Tower City.

In 1872, Tower and Munson sold all of their holdings to the newly formed Philadelphia & Reading Coal & Iron Company for $3 million, of which Tower received half. Three years later, the Towers moved to Philadelphia, where he earned an even larger fortune in the iron mines of Minnesota. What made the fortune even more valuable was that there was no income tax in the United States yet. In 1880 Charlemagne Tower purchased some 20,000 acres of iron-rich land in northern Minnesota for development. Within two years he had incorporated the Minnesota Iron Company and gained control of the Duluth & Iron Range Railroad to ship ore to his docks in Two Harbors. Not bad for a former Pottsvillian.

His namesake son was educated in the Pottsville schools before entering Philips Exeter Academy and then Harvard. The young man, Charlemagne Tower, Jr., carried on in the family business after his father's death in 1889, and later involved himself in international affairs for various Republican administrations. His first appointment as an ambassador for the United States came from President McKinley, who nominated him for the Austria-Hungary post. He then served three years as ambassador to Russia, where he designed highly ornate uniforms for himself and his staff.

This peculiar dress code was carried over after his appointment to Germany, which began in 1902. The outfits consisted of dark blue uniforms, trimmed with gold buttons and gold lace, accompanying this with sword and black hat with a white ostrich feather, a far from the normal Pottsville dress of the day, and an irritation to the more unassuming President Teddy Roosevelt. Ambassador Tower was paid a government salary of $17,000 a year during his Russian term, but out of this he had to pay all of his own housing and entertainment expenses. The rental of the Ambassador's house alone cost $12,000 a year. That is one reason wealthy businessmen are generally selected for ambassadorships, as not many people want a job, glamorous as it may be, they could ill afford. Although he had traveled throughout the world and held court with presidents and foreign nobility, Tower retained a strong fondness for his boyhood town of Pottsville.

The Ambassador was back in Pottsville to visit old friends, such as Professor H.A. Becker, his German tutor, and George Frederick Baer, the multimillionaire president of the Reading Company.

In the 1890's, Baer assumed the presidency of the Reading System, which included the P&R C&I Company, with an office in Pottsville. Tower was a corporate director, and Baer wanted to discuss the future of coal mining with his guest, and also show Tower the solid new headquarters built on Mahantongo Street, diagonal from Dr. Patrick O'Hara's office. Baer's Reading Company was part of a J.P. Morgan Trust, which by 1902 controlled 96% of all the hard coal in Pennsylvania, and the state's anthracite at that time was the principal source of home heating on the eastern seaboard of the United States. The operations that he administered did not come without controversy. Baer would be remembered for his infamous quote concerning the miners that he employed as he spoke before the Anthracite Coal Commission in 1902.

"These men don't suffer. Why, hell, half of them don't even speak English."

It was these words that turned public opinion against management in the ongoing labor disputes. He considered capitalist entrepreneurs, such as himself, to be fulfilling God's divine plan when he wrote, *"The rights and interests of the laboring man will be protected and cared for not by our labor agitators, but by the Christian men to whom God in his infinite wisdom has given control of property interests of the country, and upon the successful management of which so much remains."*

Expressions such as these infuriated President Theodore Roosevelt. In a meeting at the White House with Baer, Roosevelt angrily said, as the president, he had the power, and if need be, he would exercise it to end the long coal strike by calling out the troops, taking over the mines and run them. This event marked the first time a U.S. president had ever threatened such an action.

On a sunny March day, Charlemagne Tower, Jr. was Baer's guest in Pottsville, touring Centre Street, and inspecting some coal operations. It was one of the last sightings of these capitalist giants traveling the streets of Pottsville together.

"Your carriage awaits, Mister Baer."

"Thank you. Charles, after you," the host politely said, deferring to his old friend and guest for the day.

The horseman arrived in the front of the P&R C&I building, and the two gentlemen stepped in the waiting carriage. Baer was in good health for his 65 years; he was five and one half feet tall, with a well-poised head, featuring a beard and mustache. His almond eyes had almost an oriental feature to them. Many who knew him, said that George Baer resembled J. P. Morgan more than any other of Morgan's associates. He had a superlative degree of determination, confidence, and self-control, exhibited on one occasion when took control of the Reading system when nearly bankrupt, making it into a first class corporate power. He was the most influential person in Pottsville in 1907, yet he made his home in neighboring Berks County.

"Refresh my memory, George. What was on the site of your magnificent new headquarters?"

"It was the small wood-framed office of Squire Jim Fisher, Charles. My, you have been away much too long. Now let's get going, there is much going on in Pottsville these days."

The red brick townhouse of the Carpenter family neighbored the Coal Company headquarters to its west. This particular dwelling house of a prominent physician possessed federal style architectural elements dating from the mid-1850s-time period. The men in the carriage agreed that the most unique features to the building were the iron window railings on the second floor of the building. The same iron company that cast the town's Henry Clay Monument in the early 1850s had cast these iron gates.

"What intricate detail and iron craftsmanship in that building…a real beauty of a home. It may have also been the home of the old Judge, Tom Walker…I am not sure."

The coachman proceeded north on Third Street, and then took an eastwardly right turn down Market Street to Centre. The old coal and railroad baron had the coach stop pointing to the southwest corner.

"Major Heber Thompson is planning to construct the largest building in downtown Pottsville…Or was it his brother Lewis Thompson, or a partnership between the brothers?"

It was destined to be a six-story office building in the heart of Pottsville, the shopping center of the 75,000 people that lived within a fifteen-mile radius. Its fame, as the tallest building, would only last until the owners of the Schuylkill Trust Company constructed a larger eight-story edifice on the opposite corner in the mid-1920s. That was be on the site of the Thompson's hardware store. Major Thompson, a well-respected citizen, was the manager of the vast Girard Estate land holdings in northern Schuylkill County. He was often referred to as a renaissance man due to his Yale education and his military background. He dropped out of Yale just prior to his graduation and enlisted in the Union Army as a private in the "First Defenders," the first soldiers to respond to President Lincoln's call to duty. During his illustrious military career the Major engaged in combat under General Sherman's command during the Atlanta campaign. Thompson was captured and had remained a Confederate prisoner for over one year. After his return and discharge from the service, he became an engineer and agent for the Girard Estates, while also developing other business interests. He was the president of the Miners Bank, the oldest bank in the town, and was involved in various charitable endeavors.

"Construction on the Thompson skyscraper should begin in a year," Baer confidently told his traveling companion, "it will be another significant business asset to the community and replace those several small stores and the photograph gallery. They are all scheduled to be demolished shortly."

The men were not just discussing the building boom in Pottsville; the news of the day also was of interest. There was a rumor circulating that the Inland Waterways Commission may recommend that canals be revitalized. In fact someone had proposed connecting the rivers and bays between Boston and Beaufort, North Carolina so that normal ocean traffic may be carried on by means of the canals, if made deep enough. The boats could avoid the treacherous Cape Hatteras, and this would mean that the old Schuylkill Canal would be extended from its present terminal at Port Clinton to its former Pottsville terminal. It would mean a great boon for the town of Pottsville, beyond the wildest dreams of anyone! However both men thought these rumors would never become a reality. "Pottsville's days as a canal center are long gone and it is foolish to even believe these stories." They are both worldly, astute capitalists and have the business savvy to realize that the future lay in railroads, automobiles and possibly air flight.

Their carriage slowly continued south along Centre Street. Pedestrian traffic was fairly heavy that day, and they noticed the customers going into a new place at 14 North Centre opened by Nick Cassimates, a Greek immigrant. He operated a first class barbershop, cigar store, and shoeshine parlor with a Turkish bath as well.

"My Pottsville is getting more international as time goes by, as the number of foreigners is increasing, for better or worse."

Across the street is Imschweiler's, the favorite spot for some light refreshment. Mortimer's Dry Goods and Jewelry Stores are located on the northwest corner, and both very busy that day. They moved on, passing the Pennsylvania Telephone Company at 8 South Centre. Telephones were becoming more and more common everywhere, Pottsville included. In 1880 there had only been 45 in the whole county. The number was now way up. Historians record that Yuengling Brewery had the first one in the area, but the phone was used only between the office and the plant.

"It is grand to see Pottsville keeping up with the marvels of science and electronics. I understand that the school district plans to install telephones in the school buildings shortly. That will be an asset to the teachers and the parents."

Wildermuth's newspaper stand was open for business on the northwest corner of Mahantongo and Centre Street, and the place was quite popular, as the coal region published many different papers. Proceeding on, they pass Hotel Allan, operated by the Allan brothers, both of whom had been young athletic lifeguards at Tumbling Run not too long ago; across the street they see the famous Dives Department Store. At the opposite corner was the Miners' National Bank, the oldest bank in Pottsville.

The carriage soon slowed down to permit the two gentlemen to admire the beauty of the Gothic Trinity Episcopal Church.

"What a heavenly sight! It should always remind visitors of what Westminster Abbey in England must look like."

The cornerstone was laid in 1847 and the church had been serving the spiritual needs of the Episcopalian parishioners ever since. In 1874, a vestryman, Charles Baber, donated a nine-bell chime in the magnificent tower that poured its sweet sound over the downtown area. The two could hear the faint sound of the organist, Robert Braun, practicing on the church organ as they went by.

"What a talented genius! If music soothes the savage beast, then Robert Braun would bring peace to the entire world!"

Across the street, John Mootz, an immigrant from Luxemburg, was briskly walking towards his store at 218 South Centre Street, and he waved to Mr. Baer. Besides operating the store with his two sons, Mootz was the president of the Rettig Brewery on Market Street, and one of its principal shareholders and was engaged in a discussion with Father Frederick Longinus, the pastor of the German Catholic Church.

"He is a fine example of what America has to offer an immigrant who obeys the law, Charlemagne."

They looked over towards the east side, Greenwood Hill, and the two talk briefly about the land that is for sale. There were rumors that land developers were interested in that area of the town (named after a colliery superintendent, Lawrence Greenwood) for middle-class housing.

"That would be a boon to the area, as Pottsville needs more homes for the middle-class, if it is too grow prosperously."

Later that same year, two businessmen by the names of Edwards and Fleet, would purchase the Snyder Farm on the east side, which consisted of forty-five acres, expecting homes to be built quickly due to the demand for good housing. They would be proven correct and Greenwood Hill would be one of Pottsville's finest residential neighborhoods.

"That beautiful Milliken house is over on Greenwood Hill. It is one of the most spectacular and picturesque dwelling homes that I have seen this side of Europe."

The two gentlemen continuously pointed out both the historic attractions as well as the new construction as they proceeded on their way, but then they came to an abrupt stop at the scene of one of Pottsville's largest architectural losses. The old Miners Journal Building had been destroyed in a catastrophic fire in 1892. They stopped at its former site on Centre Street, where it once majestically stood, commenting on the impact of the loss.

"It had been the architectural jewel of the town and probably one of the prettiest buildings in the United States," Tower commented with a touch of nostalgia in his voice,

"The structure was modeled on the town hall in Bradford, England; which, itself, was modeled on the bell tower of the Palazzo Vecchio in Florence, Italy. It encapsulated the 18th century Victorian love of the 13th century gothic style."

Pottsville never recaptured the beauty that was lost in that fire. No cause of the fire had ever been discovered, but rumored that a member of the Philopatrian Literary Society had carelessly discarded a cigar and it landed in a sawdust box. "Imagine that with its elaborate sprinkler system, touted as being *fire-proof*." The two gentlemen looked over at the new headquarters of the Miners' Journal at 215 South Centre Street, but that building had no resemblance to its predecessor that was destroyed in the fire.

"How many newspapers does Pottsville now have, George?"

"Let me see, there is the Miners' Journal, The Evening Republican, The Evening Chronicle, The Herald, The Standard, The Saturday Night Review, the Amerikanischer Republikaner, and The Jefferson Demokrat…So, that's eight…unless I missed one."

Before heading up the hill to Miss Bannan's home, they proceeded south on Centre Street, as Charlemagne wants to see the home of the late Charles Atkins, at the corner with Mauch Chunk Street. The mansion was one of the earliest constructed in Pottsville; its owner, Charles Atkins, died in 1889. Atkins had been an iron industrialist who owned and operated the "rolling mill" in the town—'the Pottsville Iron & Steel Company.' At one time he had over 5,000 people on his payroll. He was the epitome of the 19th century Pottsville aristocrat.

Entrepreneurs, such as Atkins, were among the first in the United States to use anthracite coal as a fuel in the manufacture of iron and steel. This use of anthracite made Pottsville one of the leading iron centers in the northeast and gave the nation's manufacturers a boost in competition with their European rivals. His widow, Anna, was still living in the massive home. Charlemagne just wanted a glimpse of the Atkins homestead before turning around and heading back to Miss Bannan's home.

"Anna probably wouldn't remember, as I was just a lad when I saw her last. Her husband was close to my father though."

Across the street was the stately brick Frick house with its inviting porch on the far right, and at this point, the carriage turned around, heading north for a short distance. The coachman slowly made his way up the narrow part of Howard Avenue, referred to as Church Street by the old timers.

A sharp left was made at the back of the Episcopal Church onto Second Street. The carriage proceeded slowly up steep Second Street through the gate of the Cloud Home, which sits heavenly over the town, built just behind the pedestal holding the impressively high Henry Clay monument.

"The Cloud Home" has been the residence of John Bannan, who constructed the Greek revival palace on Sharp Mountain in 1850; the plans developed by his wife, Sarah. He was a self-made man who studied engineering as well as the law, dying at his stately mansion at the age of seventy-three.

Ambassador Tower planned to visit John's daughter, Miss Martha Ridgway Bannan, who resides in the family homestead with her two sisters, Mary and Zelia. Quite an intellectual, Miss Bannan devoted herself to the arts and humanities. She had written in verse and translated Goethe's poems from German into English. Of any woman in Pottsville, she was the intellectual equal to Tower and could be compared to the Greek goddess, Athena.

A Greek goddess of many talents, Athena was celebrated as the patron of musicians and the fine arts. Associated with the urbane, cultured life of a city, Athena devoted herself to seeing the progress of civilization including her patronage of the arts and literature from high atop Mt. Olympus. The Greek goddess is usually portrayed as one of the most benevolent goddesses…strong, fair, and merciful. Athena was known as one of the three virgin goddesses, referred to as virgin because they were able to remain independent, unswayed by the spells of

Aphrodite, the goddess of love, and the consequent pull of marriage and mother-hood. Romance and marriage did not feature in Athena's mythology. More than any other of the Greek goddesses, Athena remains a symbol of civilization, useful knowledge, noble reasoning, logic and wisdom. The goddess Athena reminds us that we can successfully use our intellect and creativity in the pursuit of any goal we choose.

During this post-centennial period, Pottsville had its own version of Athena in the form of Martha Ridgway Bannan, living high atop the town in the pure white, angelic Cloud Home.

The two gentlemen alighted from their carriage and proceeded up the steps to the front door, and then knocked.

"Guter Nachmittag, Herr Tower und Herr Baer. Kommen Sie bitte herein."

The sixty-six year old hostess stood in the hall with a welcoming smile upon her face. Martha Ridgway Bannan, the proper and dignified aging heiress, was definitely a class act in the area. She was born in the farm town of Orwigsburg but moved to Pottsville shortly after the county seat was moved to Pottsville in the middle of the 19th century. Her education began at Miss Allen's Academy, one of the earliest schools in the area, and then her studies continued in Philadel-phia. Always the patron of the arts, she was delightfully talented in music, espe-cially the piano. She was also an accomplished singer, and had been friends with Jenny Lind, known as the "Swedish nightingale" while she toured the United States, and who was Martha's personal houseguest at the Cloud Home. "Ole Bull" was another personal friend who stayed at the Bannan House. He was a Norwegian violin soloist of international repute. As a violin virtuoso, he was widely acclaimed for his brilliant improvisations, and for the rich tone of his play. He accompanied Miss Bannan while she played the piano and was considered one of her many artistic dear friends.

After a few brief words in the hallway, everyone followed the maid to the din-ing room where tea and cake were to be served. It was a warm March day but not warm enough to enjoy the outdoor porch, and still too early in the year to enjoy the magnificent mountain laurel and the lilac bushes that shortly cover the grounds with nature's spring brilliance. The apple orchard in the back had its trees all lined up, waiting for a few more weeks of sunshine to bud and begin bearing fruit.

From the Cloud Home, the men were given a bird's eye view of the stately home of Benjamin Bannan, Martha's uncle, located across town high atop Greenwood Hill; reached by way of the Washington Street Bridge. Benjamin had been the influential editor of the town's Miner's Journal newspaper. While having their tea, they discussed world events as well as the future of the anthracite coal region.

"Gentlemen, a new amusement park is to be built at the west end of Pottsville, in the area called, Railway Park," Miss Bannan informed her gentlemen callers, "It will provide a skating rink, vaudeville theatre, a carousel, dancing, a restaurant and a pavilion for outdoor concerts. The whole park will be illuminated at night by electricity. In addition, a professional baseball team was soon be playing in Tumbling Run Park in the Atlantic League."

"Such diversions will be good for the working class and minimize labor unrest," Mr. Baer thought to himself as Miss Bannan continued to discuss the optimism she has for Tumbling Run. Apparently the Pottsville Union Traction Company made a survey for a connecting trolley line to the upper lake, giving passengers an opportunity to circle the entire area. This will make much more land available for the park.

"I read that a modern amusement facility may be built, with chute-the-chutes, tennis courts, hand ball, and more picnic areas. The fame of Tumbling Run as a summer resort is spreading rapidly, and the paper indicates that many visitors from Philadelphia and east coast cities prefer Pottsville to either Atlantic City or other resorts."

The two distinguished houseguests heartily concurred with her observation.

"Enough of Pottsville. Ambassador Tower, please tell me of the situation in Europe."

Now asked, Tower politely discussed his duties in Russia and Germany.

"Czar Nicholas has serious problems in his Empire. There is a struggle being waged by the forces of socialism and anarchism. It cannot be underestimated and could pose a danger to the rest of the continent."

"What about the Jewish problem? How is that being handled?"

"That is another concern. Anti-Semitism within the Russian Empire has caused a tidal wave of emigration. The repression and degradation of the pograms needs to stop."

Tower then asked about the Jewish settlers in the county.

"Jews have been in Pottsville since the 1850's, and they even had a synagogue as far back as 1870, Temple Oheb Zedeck. Most of these immigrants came from Germany, and their synagogue, coincidentally, neighbored the Lutheran Church with its German Christian congregation," Miss Bannan responded.

Tower continued with his observations of the oppression now occurring in Eastern Europe, knowing that many of these Jewish immigrants were settling in the coal region, and were slowly blending into the established merchant class of Pottsville.

"I firmly believe that Russia is in for a long struggle to maintain the Imperial Empire. The Czar had embarked on a dangerous policy of crushing dissent that could backfire in the long run. As for Germany, it too had a growing problem with socialists and radicals."

Baer sipped his tea, trying his best to disguise his feelings that he has towards the mass of eastern European immigration that now made up the bulk of his mining labor force. He could not forget his embarrassing words that he spoke to a reporter concerning the low wages and dangerous working conditions that confronted the miners, *"They don't suffer. They don't even speak English."* These words would be repeated over and over again in the pro-labor press, earning him the wrath of the working class for years to come.

Miss Bannan periodically tested the Ambassador's knowledge of the German language by speaking in that European tongue, which keeps Baer out of the conversations at times.

"Excuse ich, Herr Baer."

The hostess, picking up her teacup and taking sip, mentioned—in her fluent German—how much she enjoyed Tower's two-volume study of the Marquis de Lafayette that he had published in 1895. The conversation then reverted back to the English language and the goings on in Pottsville and its long and interesting history. Recalling her journeys to Philadelphia by horse-drawn stagecoach over "the King's Highway," she also discussed boat rides along the legendary Schuylkill Canal.

Awe! The wonderous Schuylkill Canal was no more. It certainly was a topic that could be discussed for hours. Designed in the early Eighteenth century, the canal made the Schuylkill River navigable from the coalfields all the way to Philadelphia, one hundred miles downriver. The navigation system used canals to bypass shallow or rocky sections, and dams were built along the way. The horses and mules that walked along the towpaths, hugging the shoreline, pulled barges that were loaded with the coal, freight, and passengers. Upon entering or leaving a canal reach, the boats would enter a lock. There were about seventy-two of them. The double doors, located at each end of the lock, closed and the water rushed in, or the water was removed, to raise or lower the boat to the level of the next section of the canal. This system permitted canals to be dug outside the riverbed, bypassing sections of the river that was too difficult to navigate a boat on.

The Schuylkill Canal was a grand success story and for the next half-century, the canals brought millions of tons of anthracite coal, all dug by the cheap immigrant labor, to the markets of the industrial east coast. On the return trips the canals carried clothing, furniture and building material to Pottsville and other coal towns. 1859 was the most profitable year for the Navigation Company but with floods, the Civil War, and the introduction of the steam locomotive, the canal lost its glamour as the chief means of transportation. The railroads cut the price of transporting coal to below the profit margin, hoping to destroy its rival, the canal.

A typical train ride could transport the coal to Philadelphia within twenty-four hours, while it took the canal boat approximately sixty hours. In 1870 the Reading Railroad purchased the Navigation Company and began to slowly fill the canal beds. By 1891 the portion of the canal above Port Clinton was abandoned. No more canal boats headed to or from Pottsville. By 1904 the anthracite traffic had almost completely ceased and the incredible 450-foot long canal tunnel built by hand through the mountain near Auburn had also been destroyed. But as Miss Bannan and her guests spoke a few remaining pleasure boats still traversed parts of the once glorious Schuylkill Canal.

"That canal permitted many businessmen to make money…lots of money. The canal era was a good time for the coal region. It made a lot of Philadelphians and New Yorkers very, very wealthy."

After a short time, the gentlemen stood up, picking up hats and canes. They thank their hostess for her gracious hospitality. Donning their hats, they proceed down the steps to the waiting carriage for the ride back to the Mahantongo Street office building.

"Auf Wiedersehen Herr Baer und Botschafter Tower. Wieder gekommen!"

All at the Cloud Home had such a splendid afternoon, in the year following the centennial.

CHAPTER 13

▼

1909

1909 was the year of that murder, now long forgotten. I will get to that shortly, but I want to tell you more of young Robert Brown, or Braun. He was the finest musician that ever lived in Pottsville. My son and daughter took lessons at his school for a few years. I haven't seen either child in years. I am not sure if they would remember me now. Did you know that Braun just died earlier this year? My children performed in recitals and all of his pupils had to perform their numbers from memory. No sheet music cluttering the stage. Musicians are the people I admire the most, as without music, life would be a mistake. Nietzche said that I think.

There were some other notables that were busy that same year. Jack Picus, the ball player, for instance. Whether it was music or baseball, these two fellows gave it their best that year of the bizarre murder.

In the late spring of 1909, young musician Robert Brown set off to Europe with his instructor Constantin von Sternberg, where he traveled throughout Italy, Switzerland and Germany in pursuit of more advanced musical knowledge. Later in the summer, he enrolled at the Royal Conservatory of Music in Leipzig, the old world city where Johann Sebastian Bach spent the last 27 years of his life (1723 to 1750), and wrote some of his most important works—including the St Matthew Passion and the Christmas Oratorio.

The young Pottsvillian walked in the footsteps of Johann Bach, while studying under the current musical masters. Not only had Bach's fame made Leipzig famous, it had gained world-wide acclaim for its Gewandhaus Orchestra, which had its own musical heritage dating back over 150 years. Back then, Leipzig merchants founded and financed a concert society, which has meanwhile made symphony history, bringing forth one of the world's best-known and most renowned orchestras. Felix Mendelssohn Bartholdy, Arthur Nikisch, Wilhelm Furtwängler, Franz Konwitschny and Kurt Masur were all Gewandhauskapellmeisters. They left their imprint on a unique musical culture, as did Robert Brown in his hometown of Pottsville.

Brown would graduate from the Royal Conservatory of Music in Liepzig, and then legally assume his ancestral surname, Braun. He was thrilled to be strolling the streets of Bach and Mendelsohn, and playing music in the very concert halls that were once occupied by these geniuses. At the same time, he could not take his thoughts off of his hometown, far away across the ocean in the hills of eastern Pennsylvania. He longed to return and impart the insight that he had acquired through his long hours of practice in Europe. He would bring musical culture to the coal mining region.

That same spring, Jack Picus, the local Polish boy with the incredible right arm, who impressed everyone when he was starting out in Pottsville's Mount Hope section, was having his dream fulfilled at the age of twenty-five. Stepping out onto the pitcher's mound in New York City, he pitched a winning game! He led his new team, the Highlanders, to an American League fifth place finish that rookie season. The team later will be known as the Yankees. This was not bad for a young lad who had worked in the anthracite coal mines only a short time before. His first season was just the beginning of an illustrious career.

On the Fourth of July 1909, Pennsylvania celebrated Independence Day with the rest of the other forty-six states. Pottsville's festivities were held at the beautiful grove located at 14th and Mahantongo Street, just a block down from the Cullum house that had burned two years earlier. The colorful marching bands played patriotic music, and several choirs joined together in song under the direction of Professor Lotz, with flags flapping quietly in the warmth of a summer breeze.

Attorney Guy Farquhar presided over the event, with the main speaker being the newly elected Judge Charles Napoleon Brumm, who lectured on the events of 1776 and their relevance today in the beginning of the 20th century. The children present, if paying attention, could only imagine what the future held for each and every one of them. It was hard to believe that automobiles were replacing horses and people were flying in the air!

America was at peace and most likely would remain out of any foreign wars for a long, long time.

Later that summer, George Simon finished writing his confession while riding on the train. The confession was twelve pages long; the penmanship was in an inconsistent style. The sad declaration of guilt was hurriedly started in late August at the train station, while the writer waited for the eastbound train destined for Birdsboro. This quiet little Pennsylvania Dutch town was located in neighboring Berks County, approximately forty-five miles from Pottsville. The author nervously wrote down his remorseful words with hopes that the train that has just left Pottsville's Pennsylvania Station would jump the tracks and plunge down a steep bank. He wished that his life ended that way.

It would be a fitting end for a person that has just committed one of the foulest of crimes imaginable.

Before writing his dramatic admission, he had lied to his father, telling him "dear mother had gone up north to Mahanoy City for a few days to visit some friends and relatives." Mahanoy City was not too far from his former home town of Delano. To support this alibi, home repairs were actually being undertaken, and it appeared to be a good time for Mrs. Simon to get away. With Mahanoy City only fifteen miles away, Mr. Simon shouldn't worry, as the two men of the house could certainly get along without her for a few days. George promised his father that he would take care of the house while she was gone. That was the explanation that he gave his father, and as far-fetched as it seemed, the old man believed it.

When George Simon, Jr. was a ten-year-old Delano boy, he began to steal. At first he would take pennies from his mother's purse. It was easy to take just a few, as his mother never missed a couple of pennies. These pennies, however, were important to a child. They would entitle him to a few pieces of candy and his mother kept a lot of change in her purse.

"What were just a few pennies to her?"

Those pennies would slowly lose their appeal and be replaced by the larger currency of nickels and dimes that were in her purse. Since his mother never missed the pennies, logic dictated a slow progression to the higher denominations until she'd suspect that something was wrong. When that occurred George Simon would stop his pilfering ways, and apologize. It would be easy. However, mother never seemed to miss the nickels and dimes. When he began to take the large dollar coins, mother didn't miss those either.

He thought, "Maybe she wanted the money taken from her purse, to lighten her load."

When he was younger, the stolen money would be spent in Delano, Mahanoy City or Shenandoah; later, after moving into Pottsville, he could take his ill-gotten gains down to Centre Street, the business district of the city, where he could go into the various stores, especially his favorite, the large new department store called Dives, Pomeroy, and Stewarts, and buy things that he desired at the moment. He was, without doubt, impulsive, never thinking about the ramifications of his actions nor the harm that it would have on his beloved parents.

When he turned age thirteen, he discovered that mother's purse did not contain enough change to suit his needs. This would be his criminal rite of passage, the age at which he became a full-fledged forger, embezzling funds from his father's checking account at the Miners National Bank on Centre Street. He certainly evolved into one shrewd, devious teenager.

His confession note stated, "At heart, I was a good child, but an evil spirit that I could not resist, seemed to take possession of me."

Whether an evil spirit was prompting him, or just a natural born criminal disposition, George Simon continued to keep taking more and more from his parents, drawing him ever deeper into a world of inter-family criminality.

During his third or senior year at Pottsville High School, George became so skillful that he forged enough checks to nearly drain his dear parents' savings from the Miners Bank. He took $705, leaving $105 in their account that was saved for needed improvements to the North George Street house.

As time went by without any reprisal, his inner demons seemed to whisper in his ear that he should increase the pace of his wickedness. Assenting, he took a Schuylkill County bond that his parents had hidden in the house, and also borrowed money from both the Schuylkill Trust Company and the Pottsville Building and Loan Association in his father's name. Yes, he certainly was a shrewd and cunning young man. There was no stopping him; for some reason his parents were either oblivious to the missing money and the increasing debt that mysteriously appeared on their financial horizon. More likely, they simply ignored his transgressions and crimes. Later many would shake heads in bewilderment.

"Such a shame that something or someone did not stop him earlier in life. Spare the rod and spoil the child."

He now needed the money as he was courting a beautiful girl that lived on Norwegian Street. Viola Hartranft was her name, and he meant to impress her. So far, the relationship was an utter delight. She was one year older than he was but that meant nothing to him. He loved her so and he had thoughts of marriage. Once he got a respectable job, the two could settle in a nice home and raise a family.

On the other contrary, his parents believed that he was much too young to for the responsibilities of matrimony. They wanted him to attend college, which is why they tried to save the hard-earned money. A college education could be his for the asking. But most of their money was already gone, taken from them unwittingly by their selfish son.

Over the years, George's inner demons took control of him, turning his thoughts to the pursuit of evil, sin and wickedness. The struggle between the two sides of the young man continued relentlessly. When his evil impulses were under control, he would pray to God in relief. He said a prayer at the end of August; that was a certainty.

"Thank God I did not complete my wicked plans when I was alone with father."

Somehow, on the last Sunday evening in August night, George built up the courage to leave the family home. He almost finished his original plans, but some sign of conscience or some weakness stopped him. For a brief time, he felt that he was in control of his actions, rather than the inner demons. He packed his suitcase and left for the passenger station on Norwegian Street, to catch the early train to Birdsboro. He would soon be with his sweetheart, Viola. She was away on a short summer vacation and he missed her so.

George also needed to flee the house immediately for other reasons that only he knew. He could no longer stay in that George Street house, or the demons would overpower him; compelling him to finish the evil scheme that began nine days ago. Now the house possessed too many dark secrets.

He has to get away as quickly as possible. He has to get a grip on himself.

Travel plans filled his thoughts; maybe he could continue towards Philadelphia. "Viola will accompany me, of course. Wanamaker's Department Store is there, in all of its twelve-story grandeur; the grandest department store in the whole world."

Wanamaker's was the premier store in North America. It was the first department store to allow exchanges and refunds. It was the first store in the whole world that used electric lights. It had a huge organ, and concert recitals were given while people shopped. Yes, Wanamaker's would be a destination.

"After some shopping, we could continue by train to Atlantic City, New Jersey. It would be a marvelous time. I have some money to pay for everything."

After checking the local newspaper ads, he discovered that the Pennsylvania Railroad ran excursions from Pottsville to Atlantic City. The cost was only $3.25

per person, and that was the round trip fare! It will be a great ending if Viola would go with him.

"The beach is supposed to be lovely this time of year."

Atlantic City, by the late 1800's was the ideal destination for vacationers. By the turn of the century, nearly 2/3rds of the city's 6,500 dwellings were cottages with many huge two or three story homes owned by the prominent business people developers from Philadelphia and New York. Along the boardwalk, developers erected immense, elaborate hotels and amusement piers. There was now entertainment for every taste imaginable. Atlantic City had become "the place to go," and entertainers from vaudeville to Hollywood graced the stages of the piers. By 1900, more than 27,000 people resided in Atlantic City—up from just two hundred and fifty in 1855, and it was still increasing. It was such a wildly exciting place. The saloonkeepers and café owners supposedly defied the blue laws, keeping the numerous establishments open for business, despite the uproar from the clergy. Critics observed that baseball was being played on the Sabbath. It seemed to them that nothing was sacred anymore.

"Viola, Viola, please come with me," he pined to his inner self.

George Simon wished that Viola would go with him to Atlantic City, where they could both forget their troubles and woes. They could walk the boards and swim in the Atlantic Ocean, even for just a short time. They could even take a ride in a roller chair and be wheeled up and down the boardwalk. Wouldn't that be grand? He checked his wallet; there was enough money to have a marvelous vacation.

Tooot......Toooot......Toooot!

The loud train whistle sounded, breaking George's idle daydream. Soon he will be in Birdsboro. Suddenly his thoughts returned to Pottsville and his mother. He remembered how she took his hand walking around Delano as a youngster. How she taught him to read, add and subtract. She was such a wonderful mother, reading him bible stories. "Thou shalt honor thy father and thy mother," was one of the commandments chiseled by God into the sacred tablets. Moses taking his people to the Promised Land was another often-told story. "Thou Shalt Not Kill" was yet commandment. Then he thought of the New Testament story of Judas Iscariot, the apostle of Jesus Christ, who hung himself after betraying the Lord. Something inside started to tear at George's heart.

As he alighted the train his conscience continued to bother him.

Before dropping his several letters into the mailbox, his mind wandered back to his home on North George Street. He pictured his loving parents walking about in the home. He saw himself looking out the upstairs front bedroom window. Looking out the window, he saw see the beautifully constructed county courthouse and the foreboding brownstone prison situated to the rear. The prison reminded him of the French Bastille, a place where he would never allow himself to be sent, no matter how his evil his impulses became. He remembered the degradation of Charles Wartzel and Felix Radzius, both hanged in the Pottsville prison yard before a hungry crowd of his townspeople.

"I would rather be dead than be locked up in such a prison," he thought while visualizing his mother stroking his hair back and kissing him farewell.

"I hope to see you, mother, very shortly. It won't be long."

CHAPTER 14

▼

GEORGE STREET

It is difficult for me to recount that grizzly crime. It makes me sick to my stomach. I had never seen anything like it and I am sure I never will again, but I will tell you what I know about it...the best I can. Did you ever see "Dial M For Murder," the newest film starring Grace Kelly? I enjoy the movies a lot. She's from Philadelphia, you know? I saw it in 3-D, wearing those funny glasses. I love a good murder story, don't you?

Now I will follow through with the story of the alleged murderer, George Simon. As a former newspaper reporter I got used to calling every murderer or criminal "alleged" so that I wouldn't get sued for libel. It is a habit I still have, even though I have not been reporting for decades.

"What is George up to now and where is my wife?" the elder Simon wondered out loud.

George Simon, Sr. suspected that something was wrong when he returned home from his arduous work at the shops in Delano. He was certainly puzzled that his wife would travel to Mahanoy City for several days without, at least leaving him a note. Without a telephone, the possibility of contacting her was slim and he could not afford to take a day off from work.

His son, however, had offered to help around the house while his mother was away. His proposal to cook and clean was much appreciated; it appeared that George's behavior was improving.

"Yes, he has been helping around the house. Maybe we can have the man-to-man talk that we should have had years ago. He must plan for his future."

Young George was slowly becoming responsible. Maybe Mr. and Mrs. Simon were wrong in believing George to be a disappointment. His son was now attempting to be considerate for a change, a most welcomed change. Doing house chores for the first time in a long time would do his son good. George hadn't even brought up the name of his girlfriend, Viola. Maybe the puppy love romance was over? Only time would tell.

The Pottsville Police station shared its office with the Borough Hall, located downtown on North Third Street. The chief of police during the centennial era of the city was forty-six year old Hiram S. Davies, a borough native educated in its public schools. In his youth, he was a versatile athlete who excelled in handball, as well as being one of the school's finest sprinters. For a few years he had been employed as a puddler at the rolling mills of the Pottsville Iron and Steel Company, in the north Fishbach section, near his birthplace. A "puddler" was a person in charge of a furnace at a steel mill, a highly skilled and dangerous occupation, requiring physical strength, stamina and sustained concentration. After Davies' marriage, he found employment at the plumbing and steam fitting business owned by his father-in-law, George Blank, a veteran of the Civil War. A few years later, he was able to secure employment on the Police Force under the command of Chief Pritchard. Police work had been his dream. Within a short time the borough council elected him as chief of the police, a title he will hold for many more years.

Assuming the office gave him the responsibility of supervising a ten-man police force sworn to maintained law and order in Pottsville. As most police chiefs, he was active in the political arena. A life long Republican, he was considered a power to be reckoned with in the polling booths in the Sixth Ward, where he had always able to deliver the needed votes. As for his religious affiliation, Davies was a devout Episcopalian, attending St. John's Chapel in his beloved Fishbach section of town. The chapel was not too far from his home at 577 Peacock Street, and it was under the auspices of the oldest church in Pottsville, Trinity Episcopal. The Episcopal Church organist, Robert Braun sometimes played at the chapel services, which delighted the Fischbach parishioners.

The chief was a handsome man with a loving wife, Laura, who gave birth to their many children. His offspring eventually numbered fifteen. Hiram Davies epitomized Pottsville during this centennial era; he truly loved the town, wanting his large brood of children to grow up, sharing with him the same pride for Pottsville. There had been agitation over the years for a charter to "reform" Pottsville and transform it from a borough into a city. He was totally against such political activity, thinking that the system was fine in its present state.

"It's the duty of the men of the town to elect good people…Don't throw the baby out with the bathwater…If it's not broken, then there is no need to fix it." These were typical positions of those opposed the idea of a city charter.

Just before the phone rang Davies was reading over the newspaper coverage of the county election shenanigans, the Shenandoah ballot box stuffing scandal. Its latest episode was now playing itself out in the Court. The center of attention of the scandal was focusing on the recent voting in Shenandoah and the large numbers of ballots being called into question. Allegedly, 385 ballots failed to be supported by credible evidence of having been placed in the ballot box; yet the election commissioner counted them. On September 9th President Judge Shay handed down his opinion, voiding all of the votes in Shenandoah's Fourth and Fifth wards stating, "Election frauds, which are so notorious in certain districts of this county, will continue to be perpetrated with impunity and brazen effrontery and with complete immunity depriving electors of their franchise, and bringing contempt upon the administration of justice, until we shall, and with full power, to take upon the task of suppressing it…it is ordered…that the returns of the election officers for the Fourth and Fifth wards of the Borough of Shenandoah shall not be counted…"

One of the leaders to expose this blatant election fraud was William Wilhelm, the fifty three year old "progressive" attorney who had been associated with many noble causes over the years. It was in his blood, as his father, John, was an ardent abolitionist, who had the distinction of hosting John Brown and his followers on their way to their date with destiny at Harper's Ferry. Wilhelm, who lived and practiced law in Pottsville, had the task of reviewing the valuation of coal lands for the county in 1892. As a result of his astute work, the coal land valuations were increased by one hundred per cent. Wilhelm considers himself a progressive politically, and had been active in both the Greenback Party and The Keystone Party. In 1909 he led the crusade in probing the ballot box stuffing, securing the convictions and guilty pleas of twenty-four people in the county; an accomplishment unheard of in the state of Pennsylvania.

Davies intently read the latest episode of Wilhelm and the Shenandoah elections shenanigans when the telephone operator connected a frantic caller to the stationhouse; Chief Davies dropped the paper and answered the phone.

"Pottsville police station, Chief Davies speaking."

"Something terrible has just happened on North George Street."

Within minutes the George Simon, Sr., the distraught homeowner, was talking to chief in the front of his home.

"I should have known something was wrong when I got to the top of the third floor."

The Simon house was a large two and one half-story frame dwelling with a large basement. The family used the basement as a kitchen and dining room, while the first floor contained the parlor and living rooms. The second floor had the bedrooms of Mr. and Mrs. Simon, as well as the son's room—and the spare room that was used for storage. The second floor was, for all practical purposes, the third floor to the residents.

"I noticed that the door of the spare bedroom in the front of the third floor was screwed shut." He never noticed that before, but his son told him that the long awaited home repairs were finally beginning. "Painters had screwed the door shut so not to upset all of their paint and other materials inside," was what his son told him and it seemed a most reasonable answer at the time.

In fact, he smelled the faint odor of paint, or was it disinfectant, or paint cleaner? It certainly was an unusual scent. Certainly an odor he never came across before.

"What could it possibly be?"

CHAPTER 15

▼

WHAT WAS HE
THINKING?

Most of what I am telling you can be found in the newspapers. You don't need to talk to me. I certainly can add some personal flair to the one-dimensional story. There is no record of what really went on when George left town to visit his beloved Viola. I sort of fill in the missing pieces, to a degree. I am not the type to delve into the romantic or sexual relationship between those two young people. Maybe it was my Catholic upbringing. Sins, whether of the flesh or not, should be told revealed only within the confines of the confessional. Anyway, I respect people's privacy, even if one of the people is a madman, or I should say "alleged madman."

I tried my hand at writing pulp fiction during the 30s and 40s, but I never got a break. I had plans to write a book about the murder some day. It is probably too late for me. When I tell you about it, maybe you can write the book. Maybe Alfred Hitchcock can make a movie about it with Grace Kelly taking the role of Viola. Anyway, the book, whether I write it or you do, will be a unique psychological exploration into the mind of a madman, who is not an exotic monster, not a werewolf, nor a gangster, but rather the most ordinary, most mundane individual that walks among us. He is the person that you say hello to when passing on the street every day. He is so frightening because he is so much like us. He was a part of Pottsville's history, whether the city wants to remember him or not.

George placed his confession, along with two other letters, in the Birdsboro mailbox when he arrived in the quiet little town south of Reading. He was sure that the mail would arrive by the time he and Viola return to Pottsville...if they would ever go back to Pottsville.

The letters explained everything. There was nothing left to discover about him. He poured his stained soul out in those letters. For once in his life he was being honest and truthful, he thought to himself. Unfortunately, it would all have to end so very soon.

"There was no turning back now," he thought.

Viola's suitor arrived at her door and she greeted him, thinking that he seemed so distant.

"George, how I missed you. Thank you for coming. You are the tonic that I need to build up my strength," she excitedly proclaimed as she threw her dainty arms around him, "Are you feeling alright? Come in, sit down and rest here in the parlor."

She had been his sweetheart for several years and she thought she knew him better than anyone else. Viola sensed that something was wrong. Maybe the train ride upset him? He came to Birdsboro to stay a few days with her while she vacationed with relatives. The two of them planned to return to Pottsville on Thursday.

"The poor boy, maybe he is upset with her relatives?"

"He would sit for hours on his hands, without speaking a word to anyone. He mentioned that we should travel to the seashore as he some money from his uncle to cover our expenses," she would later tell the police when questioned at the station.

Viola knew that there was something wrong and she tried to get George to open up to her but he would not.

"No George, I will not go to Atlantic City with you. It is such a long ride and if the train ride from Pottsville has tired you out, then a trip to Atlantic City would only exacerbate your problem and mine. I am here in Birdsboro for some needed rest. You will absolutely love it here George. Yes, you will."

"Anyway George, Mama has arranged a doctor's appointment for me back in Pottsville in a few days. There will be another time for Atlantic City George. We have our whole future ahead of us."

As time passed in Birdsboro, Viola realized that it wasn't the train ride down that was troubling George, as instead of getting better, he seemed to get moodier and more despondent as the time passed. The clean country air of the Pennsylvania Dutch farming village was having no effect on him. He knew he was doomed, and he was doomed before he ever set foot in Birdsboro.

George dwelt on the concept of time while in Birdsboro, counting the hours and minutes. Isn't it strange how the same quantity of time, measured by a precise timepiece, can be unbearably slow and astonishingly fast simultaneously?

"What is troubling poor Georgie? I wish he would tell me."

Viola continued to worry over George during the entire visit, but after several days the young couple bid farewell to Viola's relatives, thanking them for the hospitality shown them. They boarded the train at the Birdsboro station, heading back north to Pottsville.

"All aboard for Reading, Auburn and Pottsville, Penn-syl-vain-ee-awe!" shouted the conductor. George helped Viola up the steps and they found a seat near the front of the passenger car.

The train was scheduled to arrive at 1:25 P.M. Viola found a copy of an old Miners Journal newspaper and began reading, while George just sat, staring out of the window. Viola looked at the entertainment advertisements for the upcoming Labor Day weekend.

The Academy of Music was featuring "Moulin Rouge Girls," real burlesque, featuring Milton Shuster—'the funny little Jew,' Al Belford—'the roley poley comedian,' and Joe Mack—'the Irish favorite.' Later in the week, there would be a Minstrel Show. At the downtown Slater Theatre a play was being featured, "Bell Boy Trio," plus motion pictures.

"George, dear, the seats are only ten cents. Maybe we can see a show this weekend."

She thought to herself, "he wanted to go to Atlantic City. Maybe this would cheer him up? Birdsboro was too boring for him."

"George, we can take the trolley to Tumbling Run and see Thurston. You know, he is the world's greatest magician."

Thurston was destined to be one of the greatest magicians of all time, having studied magic from the young age of seven. Despite a variety of occupations, such as newsboy, racetrack tout, carnival hanger-on and medical missionary student, he maintained his passion and interest in the magical arts. Thurston's dedication paid off, as he became an expert card performer. Making his debut as a six-dollar a week circus magician, he worked his way up through a succession of carnival and dime museums. Eventually, he became a hit in the vaudeville circuit with his specialty-card magic. At one point Thurston thirty assistants and more than thirty tons of magical apparatus, in what was surely the largest, most lavish and spectacular show of its kind ever. Thurston's success in Europe let him build an illusion show, which he took around the world. He visited Australia, India, and the Orient, polishing his skills and developing a stage presence that served him well. Now Thurston would be appearing at Tumbling Run and prices to his shows ranged from only twenty-five cents to one dollar.

"It will be a great show to see! It will be something for us to remember forever. There will never be another Thurston."

Not getting a response from George, Viola leaned over to George and stroked his hair.

"A penny for your thoughts."

George, however, still did not answer. With a long, sullen expression on his face, he stared out the train window as the train continued along the tracks to its northwestern destination. He intensely looked at a few darkened clouds that were passing by.

A vivid imagination can make clouds appear to be something other than what they are. Was one cloud now taking the shape of *Tisiphone*, the mythological Fury, the punisher of crimes?

The young man believed that he was losing his mind. On this train, at this very moment, he felt as if he was going crazy. He had tried to fight against it, but it was no use. There was no way to conquer the mental anguish that had enveloped him. He continued to look out the window in complete dispair.

"Will I end up in the insane asylum in Schuylkill Haven? I am sure that will occur, provided I am captured...taken alive? Will Viola stand by my side after I'm adjudged a raving lunatic? Doubtful, so very doubtful. She is so beautiful and some other lucky man will catch her fancy. Mother will like that, yes she will. She never liked Viola; neither did father. I want Viola for all eternity. Nothing should separate us, nothing, no nothing."

"What is he thinking?" Viola thought to herself as she watched George staring out the window, his eyes appearing to be fixated on the passing clouds, while she continued to stroke his head and hold his hand.

"Those clouds will pass George. The skies will turn blue again once we arrive in dear, old Pottsville," she thought as her eyes began to tear up ever so slighty.

Never in a million years would Viola believe what George was thinking...no, never in a million years.

"I had hoped to slay my father when he was asleep. I thank God for the courage for stopping in time. I did not complete my wicked plans. I will commence and consecrate my soul to God, and may the Lord, Jesus Christ, have mercy on me. I hope to be with my dear mother, so soon. I miss her...I miss her...Oh, how I miss her. Forgive me father, for I know not what to do."

His thoughts began to take control of him; he was powerless to stop the ugly inevitable.

"George, would you care for a gumdrop?"

At that moment George seemed to have awoke from his deep nightmarish trance, and for the few miles left of the trip the two enjoyed discussing the delights and joys contained in the simple gumdrop.

When they arrived back at the station that Thursday, the young lovers decided to walk around the downtown and then head home by way of Norwegian Street. They did not get on the trolley heading west on Market Street that leads to the People's Railway Station on Twelfth Street. Centre Street was just a short distance with all of the beautiful buildings and fine city stores situated there.

Viola said to George, "You appreciate all the fine things in life. Let's see what the stores have to offer us. We can window shop a bit and stretch our legs after that long train ride."

George obliged and the two set off by foot to do some window-shopping, with George carrying the two suitcases. The array of goods for sale in Pottsville was breathtaking—coal stoves, bread toasters, coffee grinders, wooden ice boxes, rocking chairs, grandfather clocks, and stereoscopes with slides to view—all such great additions to any household.

Centre Street was home to the best of all the shops, and they wished they had time to meander and enjoy themselves. There was Drobel & Hoffman's Clothing and Furnishings, Gorsuch Medicine Store, Seidle's Shoe Store, Hushler & Greenwald's, Bergeman's Pool & Billiard Parlor, and Hodgson's Ice Cream Parlor. Such a magical street, but it will have to wait for another time.

"George, isn't it wonderful to live in a town with so many theatres. I love the moving picture shows. I just do."

She looked up and down the street and noticed all of the theatres. The Slater Theatre, The Fairyland Theatre, The Columbia Theatrorium, The Lyric, and The Lion Theatre at Centre and Mahantongo. The Pottsville Republican newspaper referred to its town as being known throughout the nation as "the best inland city in the state of Pennsylvania" and "the best little show town in the coal region." Pottsville was truly becoming an entertainment area, as well as a main shopping center. None of these other theatres in the town, however, could ever rival the beauty of the Academy of Music.

"My favorite, of course, is the Academy of Music. I love the plush seats, the velvet tapestry and the mythological imagery. When I am in that Theatre I feel as if I am in London or Berlin."

It seemed that with the arrival of moving pictures, anyone could install a projector and show a film in any of the downtown buildings. The Lion Theatre did have an interesting marquee that lit up the words "The Lion" in electric light bulbs at night, and added a sophisticated touch to the downtown, while The Columbia offered a very respectful "The Life of Christ" when it opened in December 1907. For only ten cents, any paying patron could watch a depiction of the life of the Savior, who died for the sins of mankind, commanding his followers to "do unto others as you would have them do to you." The Academy of Music was first class and in a league far above the others.

The suitcases were heavy, although George did not complain. Viola looked at her watch and said that they needed to go home. The couple needed to pick up their step. Viola offered to help carry one of the two suitcases, but George refused the offer, as it certainly was not the role of a young lady to be doing such arduous work, especially in the outfit she was wearing. Her afternoon hat kept her shaded from the sun, but she was still warm wearing her long dress, and the walk up Norwegian would be eleven blocks—all up on a slight incline.

George's woolen jacket made his task more arduous and he perspired quite a bit. Proceeding on their stroll down Centre Street, a young Pottsville Republican reporter stopped them, asking, "Do you have the time of day?" The correspondent was in a rush as there was a big story to cover over on the east side of town. He told them that they would read about it in the paper tomorrow. Apparently this didn't interest the young lovers as they proceeded on their way. They seemed oblivious to the news of the day. Of course, that was not unusual for young lovers. So many things were happening in the world. Robert Peary had conquered the North Pole, William Taft was beginning his term as President, an income tax was being proposed for the country, and some new invention called "plastic" was being heralded in the science world. None of these events seemed important to them.

They were young and in love.

Peary's conquest of the pole was especially the talk of the town, as Pottsville lost one of its favorite sons in an earlier attempt at conquering the North Pole. On July 18, 1884, the citizens of Pottsville heard of the dangerous rescue of the six survivors from the ill-fated Greely expedition. Adolphus Greely, a lieutenant in the U.S. Army Signal Corps, led an assault that successfully reached farther north than any previous expedition. While retreating from his outpost high in the Canadian archipelago, Greely ran out of food. Arriving eight months after the ship lodged in the ice, the rescuers discovered that nineteen of Greely's men starved to death. Six emaciated survivors, including young Joe Ellison from Potts-ville, Pennsylvania, were found eating shoe leather in order to stay alive. Such an awful sight! The joy of Joe Ellison's rescue soon disappeared. Ellison did not sur-vive the amputations required by the frostbite that had devastated his limbs. Sub-sequent news reports of heroism, grisly deaths and rumored cannibalism kept the whole country riveted on the Greely saga for weeks to come. Peary referred to the Greely adventure as "a blot on American polar exploration." Yet, when Peary's triumphant conquest occurred, the people of Pottsville began leaving flowers on the gravesite of Joseph Ellison, located at the new German Catholic cemetery in Yorkville. Joe Ellison's heroic endeavor would never be forgotten. For Pottsvil-lians, Joe was a hero who had helped clear the way for Perry and future adventur-ers.

No, at that time the young couple could care less about Peary's frigid adven-tures; rather they discussed whether or not to take a trolley home after all. Potts-ville had an excellent trolley system and it was extremely popular. During the centennial celebration, the operators reported that the trolleys carried 200,000 passengers during the four days of activities, with the peak being on Wednesday September 5th when an estimated 80,000 rode the cars. The trolley system began back in 1889 by the Schuylkill Electric Railway Company, with Pottsville as its central headquarters. One could travel by trolley from Heckscherville, west of town, through Pottsville, continuing almost to the borough of Mauch Chunk, in neighboring Carbon County. The town was now so busy that an editorial in the Pottsville Republican stated "it is but a question of time before underground traf-fic, or subways, reach Schuylkill County, and all of the trolley cars and overhead wires are placed underground in passing through our town."

Deciding on not taking the trolley, the couple continued to walk towards Norwegian Street. They walked by Fred Portz's Beer Saloon, located at 122 North Centre. George briefly gave some thought to having a cold beer, thinking that it could do him some good.

"Physicians have been touting the medicinal benefits of beer, Viola."

Looking at her, he noticed her expression of disapproval. Anyway ladies dared not enter a saloon.

"Mother would not approve of me going into the saloon either," thought George.

Fred Portz operated one of the most popular saloons in the town, and he was a man with a most interesting past. This German immigrant fought in the German Army before coming to the United States. After settling in Pottsville, he became the foreman of the fermenting department at the Yuengling Brewery, a position he retained for fourteen years. In 1881, he retired from the brewery, opening his own liquor establishment. Active in politics, he was a candidate for Director of the County Poor House on the Lincoln Party ticket in 1906. That party was a reform-minded party dedicated to the goal of overthrowing the Quay-Penrose Republican machine. Its leadership had called the late Senator Quay the "unblushing champion of corruptionists." While losing the election, Portz polled a good number of votes, remaining one of Pottsville's most respected citizens. The couple greeted Mr. Portz who was standing by the doorway, and continued on their way. They would soon be off of Centre Street, heading to Norwegian.

Centre Street was generally always busy with people carrying on their daily affairs. Some of the more notable citizens could usually be seen in the crowds of the ordinary laborers. For instance, it was not be uncommon to see the elder statesman of Pottsville, Guy Farquhar walking to and from his office. At one time the esteemed former district attorney involved himself in politics, but soon became disillusioned with the rampant corruption and graft in the county. He then withdrew from the political arena entirely. After the election of 1877, Farquhar was appointed by the Court to investigate the alleged rampant voter fraud in Cass Township, a municipality to the west of Pottsville. Through his diligent effort, grand jury indictments were procured against the alleged perpetrators. Guy Farquhar was now the general counsel for a reformist taxpayers' association, engaged to secure convictions in the continual election fraud cases that some observers called "a plague upon the county." He was also representing the Law & Order Society, a group founded to curtail the ever-increasing number of saloons in the county. His supporters said that Farquhar was at the head of every good, solid and sound reform movement in the county and town, whether social or political in nature. While the barrister was one of the founders of the Phoenix Fire Company, the humble man never sought public praise or commendation for his accomplishments for the betterment of Pottsville. Many residents remembered that Attorney Farquhar, who, along with William Shaeffer, secured an old frame building in nearby Mount Carbon during an epidemic. The two men hurriedly opened the facility as a hospital for the ill and infirmed. This early success motivated Farquhar to pursue his dream of having a first-class hospital constructed within the borough. His dream would be fulfilled with the opening of the Pottsville Hospital, becoming its first chairman.

Viola was quite beautiful beneath her large hat, wearing a stylish dress covering her slim framed figure. She remained next to George's side, as they finished their walk along Centre Street. Completing the window-shopping, George glanced into the window of Seidel's Shore store, noticing all of the fine shoes that he could purchase with the money that was in his wallet…the money that he received from "his uncle." Just a short time ago, George believed that Viola would be his bride, but now too late for such thoughts. Everything was changed forever. He glanced over to his right towards the east side of town, breathing a long sigh as he thought of his home and his dear mother. Checking his coat pocket, he felt the hard metal of his pistol that he carried with him. He glanced into the window of Swalm's Hardware Store at 21 North Centre with its fine selection. Was this the place where he bought the new screws to seal up the spare bedroom at his home? Finally, the two looked into the store window of Hirshler & Greenwald's, at 10 North Centre.

Viola pointed out some of the men's wear. She told George, "we can go to the store on Saturday and I'll help you pick out a new outfit."

Little did she suspect, but George would not have an opportunity to purchase a suit after today.

Once on Norwegian Street, they stayed on the shadier side of the street. The eleven blocks went quickly, and George told her that the exercise was doing some good after the long train ride back home. Norwegian Street was a busy working class neighborhood. The narrow street was crammed neatly with row homes of the working class people of Pottsville. The couple walked on the shady side of the street for the long eleven blocks to the Hartfranft home.

Once inside the row house, George placed the suitcases on the hallway floor, and walked into the kitchen to get a cold glass of water from the icebox.

After the arrival to Viola's, George Simon's mental condition suddenly worsened.

"Viola, we need to go out after supper. There is something that I need to talk about. I should have told you about the family problem when we were in Birdsboro, but I did not. After supper, let's go to Baber's and sit by the pond and talk."

After placing the pitcher back into the icebox, Viola's mother joined the couple in the kitchen. Mrs. Hartranft was fond of George but thought he was spending too much money on Viola, and also the gifts that George gave her were totally unnecessary. Germans were thrifty people and George's extravagance was not looked upon favorably.

"George, why don't you go upstairs to the bathroom and wash up. You are all perspired carrying those two suitcases from the station."

Viola and her mother remained seated at the kitchen table, discussing the relatives from Birdsboro, when George stood up and walked out of the kitchen towards the sofa in the parlor. He sat down but found no true rest. He just thought and stared.

"I will not go to the insane asylum. No, sir. The county built the asylum, or almshouse, outside of Schuylkill Haven...placed in the rural area to remove patients from home environments...I can't see myself walking around the grounds in some sort of hospital gown...They will want me to get fresh air in a bucolic setting. They will tell me to get plenty of exercise, study, making baskets, and reading the bible. Ha! No, sir. Healthy, clean living. Ha! I must take Viola for a walk in the Baber Cemetery. Mother, do you think that I am mad? Thank you mother...Mother, do you approve of Viola now? Would you come to our wedding, mother. I will let you out of your room, if you only tell me that you approve of Viola. So, you would like to talk to her about your concerns? I think that would be a good idea. You two must get together soon."

Viola walked over towards him, interrupting his silence with her answer to his earlier question.

George, after Dr. Gillars examines me, and after supper, we shall go to Baber's and sit by the pond. You can confide in me. George, you are the love of my life."

Viola asked, "Do you want to hear some phonograph music? Music soothes the savage beast, they say."

George responded sullenly, "it doesn't matter."

Viola walked over to her mother's hand-cranked Victrola and placed on a new phonograph recording. It was a very popular tune, sweeping the nation, "By the Light of the Silvery Moon," performed by Billy Murray & the Hayden Quartette. Viola was not unlike other young women of that time, enjoying this new music, referred to as "tin pan alley music." She liked that type of music more than those Caruso records, music of her parent's generation. Viola thought that this music would relax George, who appeared to be getting more depressed sitting on the couch. Maybe she could ease the pain of whatever was bothering him, if he would only confide in her. She thought that if they married, she'd stand by him through good times and bad times, for better or for worse. While she daydreamed of matrimony, in the background the voice of Billy Murray was filling the room with cheer.

> "By the light of the silvery moon,
> I want to spoon,
> To my honey I'll croon love's tune
> Honey moon, keep a-shinin' in June

Your silv'ry beams will bring love's dreams
We'll be cuddlin' soon by the silv'ry moon..."

CHAPTER 16

▼

ACTING STRANGELY

Why didn't I return to journalism after the Great War? Well, besides my own injuries, I started to drink heavily. I thought marriage would sober me up, but I was wrong. Having a family merely gave me more reasons to drink. I had a few odd jobs, but found myself content only when I was alone with a bottle. I was a sales clerk at the local Sears, and I sold insurance. You name it and I probably tried it.

I am sure that my story on George Simon would be great pulp fiction. Maybe I would call it, 'I Dismember Mama.' What do you think? With a lurid picture on the cover, even you would reach into your pocket for the two bits to pay for it. Is that why you keep asking me more about the murder than about Pottsville's history? I admire curiosity in a person, it demonstrates an active mind.

On the other side of town, the police were still searching throughout the Simon house for more clues. The borough of Pottsville was certainly not accustomed to bizarre crimes such as the one presently under investigation. The corpse of the fifty eight year old Phoebe Simon was found inside the sealed bedroom and had been there for over a week. It had been an apparent cold-blooded murder. The nude body of the woman was laid out on the floor in a highly decomposed state, and the stench that arose was so overwhelming that the men in the room had to quickly leave. Strangely, the corpse had been soaked with some sort of lime or chemicals in a crude attempt to preserve her remains.

Some ancient Egyptians, in the mummification process, had used lime; once a corpse was dry, it would be wrapped in twenty layers of lime. The Romans, too, were familiar with the drying and preservative properties of certain chemicals. So-called plaster burials, in which lime or chalk (both drying agents) or gypsum (a natural antiseptic) was packed around the body in the Roman coffin. What did all of that have to do with the apparent murder of Phoebe Simon? What was going on in the borough of Pottsville? There certainly were no Egyptians or Roman in the area, but every clue had to be examined and discussed if the fiend was to be apprehended.

Criminal Justice was in its infancy at the beginning of the twentieth century. Blood grouping was a recent discovery, while fingerprinting was becoming more acceptable as a tool for solving crime. The use of fingerprints was replacing the old Bertillon method of body typing. That system recorded physical characteristics such as eye color, scars, deformities as well as specific measurements of the body (head circumference, height, ear size, etc). These characteristics were recorded on cards and classified accordingly. After two decades this system was supplanted by fingerprinting in the early 1900s. The Bertillon measurements were difficult to take with uniform exactness, and could later change due to growth or surgery. However, this was Pottsville and not New York or London. The police work was still conducted the old-fashioned way, but with the understanding that maybe bloody, dried fingerprints will be found and "dusted" for that new-fangled method of identification.

The sealed bedroom became Phoebe Simon's tomb, and several policemen looked around for the incriminating fingerprints. The United States Army and many police departments were collecting them to solve crimes and identify persons. Pottsville would slowly keep up with the times.

At the same moment, excited newspaper reporters from The Pottsville Republican and The Miners Journal appeared on the scene. Within twenty-four hours this late breaking story of the mysterious and bizarre death would be front-page headlines. The Journal would refer to it as one of the most hideous crimes in the nation's history.

Another policeman came into the house with his camera, photographing the crime scene. Law enforcement needed to document the house in relation to its furnishings and the victim found within. Apparently there was no trail of blood. Was the woman killed in the room where the corpse was found? Was she lured upstairs and then shot? If not, the killer did a good job of cleaning up the evidence in the downstairs. While the photographs were being taken, still another policeman took some notes as to the contents of the rooms in the house, the dimensions of each room and the conditions of the scene. He focused a great deal of attention on the bloodstains. Of course there was theory that the woman had been sexually assaulted, and that too had to be investigated.

There is much more to it than looking at a bloodstain or splatter and writing down, "This is where the crime took place." The patterns of the splatters and the shapes of the blood droplets themselves can tell how the crime was committed. Certain stains called "cast off stains" are a result of blunt force trauma such as being beaten with a hammer. Pulling back from a blow produces a blood spatter that indicates direction, by creating an arc of blood droplets. One can determine the number of blows inflicted by counting the arcs. One can also determine the orientation of the individuals involved, the size of the object used and whether the assailant was right or left handed. Any of this may help in the trial of the perpetrator, provided that he is apprehended and brought to justice.

At this point the manner of death was still unclear. It appeared to be a gunshot wound, but a knife, axe or hammer could not be ruled out. The only thing for certain was that it was no accident. What type of dark and dangerous creature would perpetrate such a horror upon poor Mrs. Phoebe Simon?

Undoubtedly the probable initial suspect was her husband. Most of the murders that occurred in Schuylkill County involved women as the victim with the husband or boyfriend as perpetrator. Wartzel and Radzius had been hanged in the County prison yard for their fatal domestic violence. Certainly good police work focused on the husband first. After the husband, other family members would be scrutinized.

The chief told his officers that he wanted the best investigation possible.

"I want a full report of her physical traits, her lifestyle, education, medical history and her last known activities. Look around and see if you can find any personal diaries or letters that she wrote or received. I want to know whom her friends were and if she had any known enemies. Get me a list of her relatives. Leave no stone unturned. Do you hear me?"

Davies decided that he would question the widower himself. Mr. Simon composed himself and sat down to answer questions. He wanted to assist the police in whatever way possible.

George Simon, Sr. began telling the chief that he believed his son's story that painters had screwed the door to the room shut. His son was a good boy, a truthful boy...most of the time. However, after his departure to Birdsboro to visit his girlfriend, the foul odor from the front bedroom seemed to become more pungent. The stench filled the whole house.

"What type of paint thinner is used in that room, and why is it taking so long for the work to be done?" These were some of his earlier thoughts. How foolish. Young George said he had accidentally spilled carbolic acid about the house, but even that would not cause such a disgusting odor. Again, he was imprudent in believing that story.

Chief of Police Davies questioned the despondent husband, asking him about his son.

"When was the last time you saw your son?"

"On Sunday he persuaded me to attend an open-air religious meeting of the YMCA, held at Agricultural Park in Mechanicsville. I had already gone to Trinity Lutheran's eleven o'clock service and heard the good reverend preach about 'The voice in the wilderness.' But, George was a very religious boy, so I went with him. While he was religious…he had done some bad things in the past, such as taking money from us. It caused us much heartache. I would rather have stayed home on my day off and rested, but I told him that I would go with him. While we were there I told him that he should try and be a better boy. I told him that his mother and I had wanted him to do well in the world. I had told him that his parents were getting on in years…He told me not to worry. He would take care of me."

"Was that the last time you saw him, at Agricultural Park?"

"No…We came home…that night…Sunday night…I do remember him acting rather strangely…"

"What do you mean, acting strangely, Mr. Simon."

"Well, I wasn't feeling well. I was worried about my wife. When I was trying to get to sleep, I felt the presence of someone in my room. I called out 'Who is there?' I could see a figure and recognized my son, George. He told me that he was looking for a match. I told him that it was late and that I had no matches. He then climbed into my bed and lay down besides me and rubbed my chest. I thought that he was lonely for his mother but I told him to get in his room and get to sleep. He got up and left for his room."

"Did you see him afterwards?"

"No. That night when I saw him looking down at me while I lay in bed was the last time. I got up Monday morning and went to work as usual. When I got home I found the note on the door."

"When he rubbed your chest, did he have a glove on?"

"I never gave it any thought. I can't say yes or no to that."

"What note was found on the door Mr. Simon?"

"It was a hand-written note that stated that all mail should be delivered to the neighbor's house until further notice. Strange, isn't it."

"You did not see your son after that time?"

"No, I did not."

"Do you know if he returned home at all after you saw him?"

"No, I am not sure. The smell in the house was getting worse and I missed my wife. I was having trouble sleeping. I was very worried about my wife's absence and the peculiar odor kept me awake. I decided to travel to Mahanoy City and look for her. On Thursday I went there and to my surprise I discovered that she was never there. I hurried back to Pottsville and got back at mid-afternoon on Thursday."

"What did you do when you got back?"

"I now thought that something awful might have happened. I had to find out what was in the spare bedroom in the front of the house. I summoned some neighbors and told them that I feared something awful had happened to Mrs. Simon. I grabbed an axe and broke into the room that had been screwed shut…I was horrified to find the decomposed body of my wife upon the floor, between the bed and the window…We ran out and summoned the police."

"Do you now believe it was your son?"

"I had no reason to suspect George, at first. My wife loved our son and he loved his mother. Why would he do such a horrible thing? He was our whole world. Now, I realize that he must be involved somehow as he had lied to me about the room being sealed by the painters."

"Do you suspect anyone else? Do you think that she was targeted by any one seeking revenge?"

"No, it had to be my son alone. He had taken money from us in the past. My wife generally kept about seventy dollars in the house. I could find no money. We also had a thousand dollar bond; that is missing too. If it had been an unknown robber, then George would not have made up the story about the painters."

"Mr. Simon, did you love your wife?"

At this point the distraught husband began to sob, "Yes, yes. I loved my wife. I loved her very much…I still love her."

"You understand that you cannot be ruled out as a suspect, Mr. Simon. When a wife dies under mysterious circumstances a husband is always considered a suspect."

"I did not kill my wife!" bellowed the widower, as he tried gaining composure.

"Did you suspect that your wife could be romantically involved with another man?"

"Absolutely not, Chief. We had a good marriage and were faithful to one another."

"Do you know where your son is at this time?"

"He was visiting his girlfriend, Viola Hartranft, who lives over on West Norwegian Street. She had gone to Birdsboro for a week or so. George missed her. I know that. Mrs. Simon and I were glad that she went away. She had some unknown health ailment…maybe migraines…I am not sure. I understand that she would be coming home to see her doctor. We hoped George would get over her. He was too young to get seriously involved. She was supposed to come home this week. I think today even, or tomorrow…I can't remember what George had told me."

"Where did you say that his girlfriend lived?"

"West Norwegian Street…the eleven hundred block."

The chief turned to Officer Graeff who had walked in during the interrogation, and said, "We better get over to 1110 West Norwegian Street right away. From the looks of things, we are dealing with a madman."

Officer Graeff nodded to the chief in affirmation.

"You said to look for any letter or diary. I found this letter in today's mail, postmarked from Birdsboro and addressed to the older Mr. Simon. It appears to be a confession and a suicide note, chief," Graeff told the chief, as he handed over the key evidence found.

Graeff then thought of the quieter times of being a police officer in the past, such as providing light for the city at night by climbing the oil lamp poles and lighting them with a torch. Now he had to deal with an apparent psychopathic murderer loose in the town

"What in the world is Pottsville coming to?" the officer muttered to himself.

CHAPTER 17

▼

A DOUBLE FUNERAL

As I told you, I actually wrote a few stories for the Black Mask and Dime Detective magazines. "Pulp fiction" is what those magazines are referred to. I got paid by the word, and never made enough to classify myself as a professional writer. My first calling was to be a political journalist, but that fell by the wayside. I then wanted to write history. That is why I have so much material on Pottsville. I never did write any history though. History has too many facts. I spend most of my time reading mythology, both Greek and Roman. When you think about it, a lot of history is based upon mythology and fable. Don't you agree?

Viola Hartranft was happy to be home, and to have George with her. After her doctor visit and a short nap, she and George could walk to the cemetery and sit by the pond to discuss his family problems. She had been gone for over a week and needed to see her doctor. In fact, Dr. Gillars was coming over shortly for one of his house calls. He had left his office at 313 West Market Street and was heading over to her home. House visits were $2.00 if made after 6 P.M. so unless an emergency, earlier appointments were preferred. He was bringing the medication that she needed.

"I will tell Dr. Gillars that George's behavior had made more more edgy. Maybe the good doctor would talk to George and find out what was wrong," she thought.

The forty-three year old family doctor was not just a typical physician in Schuylkill County. He had an illustrious past; for instance, Gillars had been a former prison physician at the county jail for twelve years. He then ran for, and was elected to, the post of county coroner in 1901, he was coroner during the Great Anthracite Coal Strike of 1902, and held the inquest after the death of hardware store owner Joseph Beddall, despicably killed in Shenandoah in July of that year, ruling that death was a homicide. He also held the inquest after the death of the civilian killed by the soldier after martial law was declared in Shenandoah, again ruling that the cause of the civilian's death was homicide. This set off a legal battle that ended in the state Supreme Court. Gillars had always resided in Pottsville. Surprisingly, he studied to be a molder at the Fishbach Mills, not far from where Chief Davies resided, but soon he followed through on his dream to study medicine, and entered Jefferson Medical College in Philadelphia. After a very short period of time, practicing in the coal patch of Gilberton, he relocated his office to Pottsville. Dr. Gillars would once again be thrust into the limelight after visiting Viola.

The vacation in Birdsboro helped a bit, but Viola still was feeling anxious. She was so pleased that George stayed with her during her difficulties as she struggled with her health problems. He would make a fine husband. She wanted the approval of his parents so badly. The young couple had set no wedding date, even though they considered themselves informally engaged to one another. Viola hoped that Georgie's parents would be more accepting of their relationship, but so far they still were opposed. George said he wanted her to visit with his mother when she returned from Mahanoy City. She knew that it would take some more time before his parents would accept her as a future daughter-in-law. Viola thought that she could get employment. Retail jobs were now rapidly opening up for women. In 1870 only a handful of women held retail jobs, while the 1900 census evidenced this rapid rise in female employment opportunity. There were now over 142,000 women in the retail profession, and that number was quickly increasing. Sales work in one of Centre Street's fine shops or stores was a great opportunity for her to explore, she believed.

"ring, ring, ring."

"I'll get the door, Viola. It must be the doctor."

Dr. Gillars, noted for his faultless bedside manners, was a welcomed sight when he arrived at the Hartranft house that Thursday. Viola's mother answered the door, and he conversed with her briefly before giving Viola a quick examination. He then handed his patient the medication that he had promised. The good doctor had been treating Viola for her problem for approximately eight months. He thought that she was progressing nicely in her recovery. He then recommended that she try her best to relax.

"Get plenty of fresh air, and eat healthy vegetables."

He then bid good-bye to Viola, George, Mrs. Hartranft and Mr. Hartranft, who had since joined the others in the parlor room.

"Viola, when can we go for our stroll?" George asks his beloved.

"In a short while, George, just please be patient. It will be a beautiful night out tonight. Let's not rush. Didn't the walk up Norwegian Street tire you out? The suitcases were so heavy," was her response.

Viola headed into the bathroom, placing the patent medicine, just given to her by the good doctor, next to her combs, perfume and curling iron.

George again started to brood silently. "No, they wouldn't put me away in the county asylum. No, they'd send me away with the criminally insane. I would be labeled a deviant or sociopath, and sent away. They'd send me to Philadelphia or Lancaster; I am not sure where. It would be so far away, so far away from Viola. No! They will not separate us! I won't let it happen!"

No sooner than after the doctor left, a police car came to an abrupt stop on the block located next to the Yuengling springhouse, where the local brewery got its water supply. Officer Graeff quickly opened the door of the police car, and out jumped Deputy Coroner Carlin, as well as Chief Davies. A curious Mrs. Hartranft put her head out of the door, curious as can be after hearing the automobile come to a halt.

"Why Chief Davies, can I help you? Is there something wrong?"

"Mrs. Hartranft, yes there is something wrong. We are trying to locate George Simon, Jr. I understand that your daughter keeps company with him. Is she home or available by telephone so that I may talk with her? It is quite urgent."

"George is my daughter's soon-to-be fiancé. Did something happen to his mother while she was away in Mahanoy City? Georgie had told me that she went away for several days and he misses her so much…"

"Mrs. Hartranft, I need to talk to him immediately. I also fear that your daughter's life may be in danger. Tell us where he is! We have no time to lose."

The lovely Viola Hartranft was still in the parlor, resting on the couch. She quickly got to her feet to see what the commotion was outside.

"Who was mother talking to now?"

The now extremely nervous George, meanwhile, sprang from the sofa, and strutted across the room to the hallway. The chief now was able to see a glimpse of a male figure walking away down the hall of the Hartranft home.

"Halt!"

But George gave them no time to make an arrest as he reached into his coat pocket, pulling out his pistol. Within seconds, he placed it against his head. Only one shot was sounded. Viola collapsed when she heard the pistol go off in the hallway, as George ended his tortuous life. Joining Viola on the floor was her mother, who collapsed at the sound of the gunshot.

The police chief and Officer Graeff, with guns drawn, crouched down creeping inside the doorway towards the hallway, passing by the two women on the floor. They found George Simon, Jr. but too late to question him. He was already dead of a single bullet to his temple. His body lay perfectly still in a puddle of blood with the pungent scent of gunpowder flowing upwards around him.

When the investigation and inquest were completed, Chief Davies held a press conference at the stationhouse on Third Street. He read his prepared statement before answering questions from the reporters hungry for more information on the grizzly deaths.

"George Simon, Jr. was the sole assailant of his mother, Phoebe Simon. There are a few theories of what exactly happened. One theory is that a struggle ensued in their North George Street home. A blood soaked hatchet was found in the downstairs under the table, the weapon that killed the woman. It is believed that either Mrs. Simon caught her son stealing money from her. The boy robbed his parents over the years and left them almost destitute.

These two also could have been fighting over his relationship with the Hartranft girl, who Mrs. Simon detested. An argument ensued and as a result she received several fatal wounds from a hatchet, which we have as evidence, as she lay unconscious on the parlor floor. Another, more plausible theory, is that the crime was premeditated and the son waited for his mother to come into the parlor where he killed her by surprise. The son then removed the clothing from the victim and carried the corpse up to the front third floor bedroom, where he poured carbolic acid and lime over the corpse in an attempt to preserve her remains. It should be noted that embalmers remove bruises with bleaching agents, such as "Bruise Bleach," a compound of carbolic acid. In ancient times bodies were dipped in lime as a means to preserve them especially during times of epidemics. There was no evidence of sexual assault.

Simon then closed the windows and methodically sealed the door shut with screws. The young man apparently suffered from a split personality. Most of the time, he was a good boy, but at other times he became a criminal. He was a thief, stealing from his family. This evil personality enveloped him, causing him to commit matricide. But he wasn't finished as he planned to kill his father while his father was sleeping. He may have planned to go back and finish the job. The police found oily sheets in his bedroom and there is other evidence that he planned to set fire to the house to conceal the homicides. The son had five gallons of oil delivered to the house prior to his mother's death. This leads to the conclusion that his plan of killing both of his parents began well before the actual homicide. He would kill both of his parents and then set fire to the house. He would 'escape' and then tell the authorities that he tried to save his parents but he was too late. He then abandoned his plan to kill his father and left town. We also have reason to believe that he may have intended to kill his fiancé and then end his own life but his plans were somewhat thwarted when we arrived at the Norwegian Street house. He only was able to take his own life. There is absolutely no indication that anyone else was involved. Mr. George Simon, Sr. was not involved, nor was Viola Hartranft. Both of these unfortunate people were intended targets of the criminal mind of George Simon, Jr. He had committed one of the vilest crimes imaginable in western civilization—Matricide."

When asked about a note mailed to George's father, Chief Davies responded to the reporter that three notes were found. One was a general confession and a story of his life. The second was a letter to his girlfriend, while the third was a letter to his father. All three clearly evidenced that the writer of the notes was the sole perpetrator.

The police had also gathered the physical evidence to present to the coroner at the upcoming inquest. A sharp-edged hatchet was found beneath a carpet, together with a pair of young Simon's gloves found under the bureau. The hatchet had been wiped off, but still had traces of the victim's blood on the edge and sides. The appearance of the gloves indicated that they had been used slightly but contained no blood traces. The parlor carpet contained a large bloodstain and was the likely location of the heinous crime.

The deceased mother and son had a double funeral from their home on North George Street. The services were kept as secret as possible as the grief-stricken Mr. Simon wanted to avoid any more publicity. Mr. Shoener, a local undertaker, took the remains of the two back to the home after embalming and preparation. A few friends of the family assembled to say a few prayers for the departed souls as the Lutheran minister officiated. Reverend Reiter of Trinity Reformed Church gave a very brief sermon and then the pallbearers, chosen from among the distraught family, escorted both caskets to the waiting hearses.

The two funeral vehicles led a procession down George Street to Norwegian Street, and thence westward to Centre Street, where a southward course led them to the Union cemetery in nearby Cressona where two fresh graves awaited. Curious onlookers lined the streets in large numbers as the procession passed. Few, if any, comments were heard, as the horror of the crime was still fresh in the minds of the anthracite coal community and the sadness and shock still gripped them all.

The burial of mother and son occurred as a drizzly rain fell on the small group that had gathered to hear the clergyman recite the words from the Common Book of Prayer:

"Earth to earth, ashes to ashes, dust to dust; in sure and certain hope of the Resurrection into eternal life."

As the cortege moved away the sound of the shovel throwing the dirt on the caskets could be faintly heard.

Such a very, very sad sound.

CHAPTER 18

▼

THEORIES

When I returned from Europe, besides the medical attention for my damaged left leg, I was treated for a mild case of shell shock, often referred to as "war neurosis." That is a breakdown of the individual's rational defenses and abilities to deal with fear and anxiety. It seems that everyone has a psychological interpretation for every problem known to man. Some of these experts overlooked the mud, the hunger, the fatigue, the dampness, the lice and the rats that we doughboys were confronted with. I overcame my problem by laughing at myself and not taking myself too seriously. Of course, I had the help of the bottle when the laughing didn't work.

In any event when George Simon was laid to rest in the graveyard, the so-called experts came out in full force with their own interpretations. When I finish, I am certain that you will have your own ideas. You too can then be called an expert.

A few days later, at the Pottsville Club a few of the patron businessmen and professionals discussed Robert Louis Stevenson's novel, *Jekyll and Hyde*, over a card game in the longish room reserved for such activities. The book portrays, in simple terms, the concepts of 'good' and 'evil' and raises several interesting philosophical questions.

"Is each and every one of us born with a combination of the two concepts?" "What actions make people tip the balance one-way or the other?" "Are we predestined to do good, or do evil?"

One man at the table emphatically stated to the others that all people have the same emotions, some good and some bad and, like Hyde, when you follow the evil emotions you are considered evil yourself.

"Jekyll and Hyde both have these 'evil' emotions but what makes Jekyll 'good' is that he represses them, Jekyll is driven by reason whereas Hyde is driven by desire, he'll do what he wants when he wants. George Simon was classic case of this Jekyll and Hyde complex. He could not repress the evil tendencies that are within all of us."

"Hogwash!" responded a portly coal operator. "Children need to learn the true value of a dollar at an early age. George Simon was a spoiled child who was pampered by his parents. Children who make mistakes should be quickly reprimanded, as they must be taught to understand the real world of work, morality and struggle. They must be taught self-reliance and that frugality is a virtue. If this occurs at a tender age, then the child will grow up with a strong sense of morality and a healthy mind."

One doctor, who had just finished his meal, leaned back and lit up his cigar, interjecting his newly learned psychiatric information, also a science still in its infancy. "In 1899, Sigmund Freud published The Interpretation of Dreams, in which he studied a great number of dreams, including a number of his own, to provide clues to the working of unconscious and repressed desires. According to Freud, hysteria and neuroses were caused by repressed desires, which were often sexual in nature."

The doctor, threw his match into the nearby brass spittoon, took a puff on his Havana, and continued with his theory. "On the psychosocial level, Freud considered homicide and suicide to be the result of a conflict between one's libidinal motivation to kill a loved and hated object. In this case the object was Phoebe Simon. George became overwhelmed with guilt for what he did to his mother, the real object of his love. George was fixated on his mother, and considered his father a rival for her affections. After killing his mother, he hid her body. She was now his. He wanted to kill his father, but could not due to the mental instability engulfing him, the inner struggle between what Freud referred to as the 'id' against the 'super ego.'"

"Hogwash, doc. It may sound impressive, but I consider it pure dribble, I suggest that you stick to diagnosing liver ailments. You'd find a lot of patients in here then," the heavyset coal operator sarcastically retorted, as he collects the cards on the table.

"Can I deal you in, or does your super-ego tell you not to play?"

"No, thanks, I have house calls to make. I know what you mean, though. Freud is gaining in popularity, and his way of treating mental illness is called psychoanalysis. You will hear much about it in the future. However, I would bet that if an autopsy had been performed, then brain damage would have been found. Brain damage is the cause of most mental disorders."

A factory owner stopped at the table, chiming in with his opinion before heading down the stairs, "I am glad that he killed himself, sparing us the anguish of a public trial, although we could have all watched the hanging in the prison yard. Ha! Ha! Remember that Borden girl up in Massachusetts? It happened almost twenty years ago. Do you remember the grim poem written in her "honor?"

> *Lizzie Borden took an axe,*
> *And gave her mother forty whacks,*
> *When she saw what she had done,*
> *She gave her father forty-one. "*

An attorney, sitting at the table waiting for the cards to be dealt out, ignored the last comments, and shrugged his shoulders. He was carefully rolling a cigarette of his own, pouring the tobacco from his leather pouch into the thin paper on the table. Once his mission was accomplished he placed the cigarette between his thin lips and lit up. Taking a long puff, then blowing out three rings of smoke, he methodically set the cigarette into the ceramic ashtray found on the mahogany table. He looked up and began to state his own opinion.

"A simple a case of pure premeditated murder, it was. The young man wanted money and would do anything to get as much money as possible; even kill his own mother and father. He had this all planned out. I heard from sources that he purchased the large quantity of oil before killing his mother. Not an act of rage, as he had to go down to the basement and bring the ax upstairs. He had to put on his gloves and then wait for his mother to come into the parlor. If it were simply rage, then he would have used a weapon that was close at hand...or he would have used his hands. He had a motive. One of the oldest motives in the world—g-r-e-e-d! The lad was beneficiary of the two life insurance policies and would have inherited several thousand dollars after their bodies would be discovered in the ruins of the burned house."

"Whatever caused that Simon boy to lose his mind," said the third at the table. "It will be a story that will long be remembered, probably for the next hundred years or so. By the way, he was in that high school glee club, I think his instructor was Robert Braun. He may have gone by the name Brown back then. Whatever happened to him, does anyone know?'

"You mean Brown. He's still in Europe. Yep...he is touring France and England. He says he will be coming back to the States next year. I believe that will be coming back to Pottsville. He was dating the daughter of the newspaper publisher."

The conversation abruptly changed to America's pastime and other current events.

"Say, let's talk about our baseball star...you know...Jack Picus...He goes by the name Jack Picus Quinn now...The Highlanders are in Fifth place in the American League...I think he has a good career ahead of him..."

Yep, he sure does."

"What did you think about that sentence Judge Brumm gave that young Irish girl, Mary Kane? She got four years for robbing Tom Beddall of $175 and some jewelry here on Mahantongo Street. I think she was only fourteen years old...sixteen at best. Tom Beddall, what relationship was he to the Beddall boy that was murdered in Shenandoah during the strike of 1902?"

"I think next Saturday is ladies night here at the club. Isn't it? Or is it two Saturdays from now? "Ed Brown and his Colored Quartet" are supposed to entertain. You know that is a damn, good orchestra! The food should be great as Wimbley of Philadelphia is going to cater again."

The cards were again shuffled, flapping together, making a delightfully whirling sound, and then dealt out.

As the pile of cash in the center of the table appeared be getting larger, silence set in, and the gentlemen resumed their game in earnest. For a few moments there is nothing more important than the secrets held in one's hand.

PART III

CHAPTER 19

▼

POTTSVILLE BECOMES
A CITY

Upton Sinclair published his great novel, The Jungle, in 1906. That was the year I started as a very young journalist in Pottsville. He was an inspiration to me and I wanted to be a great political journalist. I would have wanted to win the Pulitzer Prize if it had been given in those days! I know a lot about the nasty fight surrounding Pottsville's attempt to become a city. That was part of my beat at the paper in those days.

I think it was Plato who once said, "One of the penalties for refusing to participate in politics is that you end up being governed by your inferiors." He was right you know.

Roman Emperor Marcus Aurelius was quoted as saying, "Time is a river of passing events, and strong as its current; no sooner is a thing brought to sight than it is swept by and another takes its place, and this too will be swept away." The mining town of Pottsville would see some rapid changes occur and the sweeping away of traditions and some prominent figures in the next several years.

In the summertime of 1910 Jim Jeffries came out of retirement attempting to wrestle the heavyweight boxing championship from the black hands of Jack Johnson, the first Negro to hold such a title. Thought impossible that such a thing could ever happen. The greatest sports battle of the young American century left the championship crown with Johnson retaining the crown, making that topic the talk within every barbershop and saloon in the anthracite coal region. However politics still remained the number one topic of conversation that summer in Pottsville.

The 1910 election brought with it another vote on the proposed city charter; the seventh attempt in Pottsville's history. The county seat, with its population projected to reach twenty thousand or higher within the next decade, was not unlike the whole county in general. It seemed that there was an allergic reaction to any dramatic change. It was that way one hundred years ago and it still is that way today. Both major papers in town came out strongly in favor of the Charter. The Miners Journal, now owned principally by its editor, H.I. Silliman, bemoaned the fact that the police were required to annually solicit members of the council to retain their positions; also, the fact that assessments were not uniform, but done by each separate ward. Supposedly, the charter vote was to be a nonpartisan issue, but the Yorkville Democratic Committee came out unanimously against the charter. Also, the charter opposition received much of its financial backing, supposedly, from the town's saloons. Such a very bitter and hard-fought election, but in the end the charter won by a mere seventy-one votes. The opposition had its strength in the town's sixth and seventh wards. When the final vote was tabulated, the press announced that Pottsville would soon be a third class city. Some supporters boasted that Pottsville would soon be the third major city in the state by 1920, following behind Philadelphia and Pittsburgh.

The charter vote was not the only election gathering attention, as there were national and state elections too. The unflappable Cornelius Foley was running for Congress once again that year. The sixth and seventh wards of Pottsville would be good to him and he would claim almost 20% of the total votes cast. Not bad for the young, wavy haired, downtown barber running on a shoestring budget. He spent approximately $110.00 while raising $123.00. His campaign ended up with a surplus of thirteen dollars. He captivated the attention of the voters with his outspoken candor. Traveling about the county he spoke to audiences in churches, halls, barrooms, schoolhouses, and firehouses, telling his audiences what he thought on all of the issues. There was scarcely a hamlet in the entire county where he had not spoken on a street corner. He feared no man or group of men. Even when the crowds appeared hostile, Foley persisted, explaining his thoughts with bitter sarcasm. In the most forceful language, peppered with sly innuendoes, or even open charges, he lashed out at his opponents unmercifully. On occasion he resorted to his physical prowess to protect himself from violent attacks. Despite the seriousness of the socialist platform, even some of his critics confessed that some of his remarks were humorously refreshing. Many of his impromptu remarks even gained him front-page coverage in local papers.

"If elected I will introduce a bill to take the statue erected honoring our late Senator Matthew Quay from the capitol and place it in front of the Eastern Penitentiary where it belongs."

Foley, who campaigned vigorously in several elections, would have his last hurrah in the 1912 election, running for the Congressional seat that eluded him since 1906. He campaigned relentlessly, giving soapbox speeches on street corners and halls throughout the county, but his final numbers in 1912 were substantially less than his high achieved in 1910. That year, in reality, was his last hurrah, with 1912 only a faint, distant echo. The socialists had the rug pulled out from under them in 1912 by Theodore Roosevelt's Bull Moose Party, which attracted the progressive voters away from the more frightening socialists led by Eugene Debs. Debs, if you remember, appeared on stage with Foley in 1906, and Debs' popularity kept increasing nationally. Things were different in Pennsylvania, though. The insurgent Roosevelt overwhelmingly won the Pennsylvania Republican primary, despite the Penrose machine's all-out support of the incumbent President Taft. Schuylkill County and Pottsville then supported Roosevelt in the general election when the former president bolted from his party and ran as a "Bull Moose."

CHAPTER 20

▼

A MAYOR ELECTED

I consider muckraking journalism to be a noble profession. I prefer to call it investigative journalism. Exposing fraud, waste and corruption and other evils in government were goals that I had hopes of attaining. A good progressive journalist would have no qualms in taking on the bossism, the profiteering, and political corruption that seemed to permeate throughout every aspect of public life in those days. I wanted to find muck and then rake it. I considered myself an idealist in those years before the war. I don't anymore. I signed a peace treaty with reality after the Great War ended. I replaced my addiction to idealism with an addiction to alcohol, and I am not sure which one was worse.

In 1913 the Philadelphia Athletics won the World Series and the 16th Amendment to the Constitution authorizing a national income tax was formally ratified. Both of these were of interest to Pottsvillians. Certain local developments rippled through the new little city that would also have lasting impact. For instance, in late spring, Charles Napoleon Brumm faced impeachment proceedings brought by the city barber, Cornelius Foley, his old archenemy.

"Judge Brumm is neither competent nor fair. He must be removed from the bench before any more damage is done to our judicial system."

Noted Philadelphia attorney, Thomas W. Barlow, represented Foley and proudly proclaimed to the press, "It is time for members of the bar to come to realize that some action is needed to curb the powers of the judges. "I admire Mr.

Foley for the courage he has displayed and I am determined to help him in his cause. Judge Brumm is not the only judge that needs to be investigated, nor is Schuylkill County the only county that has this problem. If members of the Schuylkill County Bar were not so cowardly…if they would simply act together for justice's sake, then it would be an easy matter to rid the courts of such offending judges. I cannot understand why the Schuylkill County bar has allowed this behavior to go unchecked."

One of the charges against Brumm was that he had handed down a four-year sentence to a young teenage girl for her first conviction on a theft charge. She robbed the Mahantongo Street home of Tom Beddall, who was a member of a prominent county family, as well as a relative of the unfortunate Joseph Beddall, the hardware store owner murdered during the 1902 coal strike. The young Mary Kane from St. Clair allegedly committed several thefts in the past, but was allowed to go free due to her tender age. Some of these prior acts included taking huckleberries from other girls. Prior to her sentencing, she was imprisoned for approximately four months. The sentence caused her so much anxiety that she committed suicide in the jailhouse by eating roach poison within twenty-four hours of her court sentence handed down by Brumm, who gave her quite a tongue-lashing. Foley blamed her unfortunate ending directly on Judge Brumm, who he referred to as "the branding iron judge," although Brumm conferred with the other members of the court on the case prior to imposing sentence.

Other charges levied against him included bias against criminal defendants despite the constitutional right to be presumed innocent. One witness testified that Brumm actually stepped down from the bench to sit and confer with a prosecuting attorney during one criminal case. Outrageous charges such as these gave the state press a field day.

"I was in Congress five terms and elected a judge while I was a sitting Congressman. I admit that I occasionally leave the bench during court proceedings but that is only to be able to hear the witnesses better. My deafness, caused from my civil war service, causes me to speak loudly at times but not at all to be rude…Schuylkill County had the worst criminal calendar in the entire state! Schuylkill County had more liquor licenses than any other county! The ballot box stuffing was notorious throughout the state! Elections in many areas of the county were a farce! Good citizens would not even bother to vote due to the fraud committed. The jury system was corrupt. The jury commissioners rigged the jury pool. I did not think that it was right that the preponderance of foreigners should make up the jury pool since these foreigners also make up the majority of those accused of crimes."

The impeachment hearings ends up costing the state $60,000, during which time rumors circulate that the judge will tender his resignation, but in the end, Brumm survived the impeachment hearing by a three to two vote. The judge apparently made a good impression before the panel investigating the scandalous charges. Surviving the most rancorous political battle of his professional life, he lives out his final years sitting on the bench of the Schuylkill County court. He remains one of the most memorable and controversial public figures in local history.

Brumm's nemesis, Foley, was not as lucky; later that year, the fledgling Socialist Party expelled him for "conduct unbecoming a socialist." What that means was never fully explained.

Robert Braun became the husband of Frances Zerbey in mid-June, 1913. His bride was the daughter of the Republican newspaper publisher. A Methodist ceremony before six hundred guests was followed by a reception at the home of the bride's parents at Howard and Fifteenth Street, not to far from the Cullum house, since rebuilt and reoccupied after the devastating 1907 fire. Frederic Gerhard performed musical numbers on his violin at the reception accompanied by a variety of distinguished talent from near and far.

Earlier the same day as the reception, seventy-one year old attorney Guy Farquhar died engaged in what he loved best, trial work in the courtroom. He died within one half hour notwithstanding the prompt medical attention he received. Oddly enough, Guy Farquhar had been born on the site where the majestic courthouse was erected. His death occurred at the same location, as if he had come full circle in the city that he loved so dearly.

While the voters in the election of 1910 approved the charter, it took years to have a mayor sworn into office. On December 1, 1913, the long-awaited ceremony took place. Pottsville was now a third class city of the Commonwealth of Pennsylvania with its own elected mayor. The hold up was attributed to the "special vested interests" that ran the town in the past, according to the Miners Journal newspaper editor. While both the Journal and Pottsville Republican newspapers supported the charter movement enthusiastically, the two papers took opposite positions when it came endorsing a mayoral candidate. The "nonpartisan" election pitted Republican John Conrad against Pierce Mortimer, the young Democrat newcomer. The Journal came out strongly for Mortimer, pleading for voters to reject the "Zerbey newspaper candidate," sarcastically referring to Conrad.

"Pierce Mortimer is...one of the strong men in the community...His name is synonymous with honesty...he is opposed to the little, inside ring rule that has prevailed

here so long, that little inside ring that has slopped in the public crib until it has grown sleek and fat—and rotten. He is here to smash it up. If elected…he will insist that all forms of petty grafting cease. The tickle-me, tickle you system will go!" He is opposed to the present rule in the police department…he is opposed to it and if elected he will do away with it…The chief of police will have to wear a uniform and tend strictly to his duties…"

The Journal came out strongly against Chief of Police Davies, who was actively supporting Conrad, a town justice of the peace for sixteen years. The paper implied that Conrad was a puppet of Davies.

"Just because Conrad was kept in power for sixteen years by the Republican Party, he know thinks that the Party should keep him in office for the rest of his life. That is the base of partisan politics. A certain group gets in and stays there. They may be incompetent or undesirable in many ways but they have a grip on the election machinery and manage to survive…Conrad is a pawn of the special interests and must be defeated…and Davies must go as police chief. Davies has been electioneering almost continuously for Conrad for the past four weeks. During this time the borough has been paying him his eighty dollar per month salary."

The day after the votes were counted, Pierce Mortimer was proclaimed the first mayor in the city's history, receiving 1,871 votes to Conrad's 1,707. Shortly after his swearing in on December 1st, Mayor Mortimer ordered the police to begin vice raids on the bawdy houses and illegal gin mills on North Railroad Street. Soon more raids occur in the Minersville Street area. The bawdy houses and illegal speakeasies that had operated in the shadow of the courthouse were exposed to the scrutiny of the press. The newly appointed chief of police, Hoepstine, conducted the raids with the approval of the new city administration. Thirty-year-old Mortimer was the youngest mayor in Pennsylvania, and he had vowed to take the city in a new direction, sincerely believing what the Journal had proclaimed in bold headlines, "Pottsville is a city of almost limitless possibilities!"

In Greek mythology, Muses are goddesses that preside over arts and sciences. Melpomene is the muse of Tragedy, represented by the tragic mask of Greek Theatre. She was visible in Pottsville's Academy of Music. Lord Byron wrote of Melpomene, "All tragedies are finished by a death…" 1914 in Pottsville would be the year of Melpomene. It would be a year of tragedy. The Muse would walk out of the Academy, with her garland, club and a sword and head towards Tumbling Run, the magnificent resort that attracted crowds from near and far. Tumbling

Run would be no more; the Railroad and Coal companies evicted everyone from their legally owned property, drained the lake and threatened criminal arrest of anyone daring to trespass. This process had already begun in 1912 and was now complete. Pottsville would never have such a natural playground ever again. No more boating, no more swimming or skating and no more theatre. "The Golden Age of Tumbling Run" was over forever. After that Melpomene called upon Thanatos, the mythological god of death to swiftly take one of Pottsville's most beloved citizens in the prime of his life. Poetically, Thanatos might be referred to the "Brother of Sleep" and the "Son of Night," but no matter how he is described, he is a creature of bone-chilling darkness. The taking of his victim saddened the new city to no end. Then when that task was completed and the life of his victim snuffed out, Melpomene walked back to the Academy and declared that she did not want to be in the building anymore. Her wish would soon be granted.

"But oh Melpomene! thy lyre of wo—
To what a mournful pitch its keys were strung,
And when thou badest its tones of sorrow flow,
Each weeping Muse, enamoured, o'er thee hung:
How sweet—how heavenly sweet, when faintly rose
The song of grief, and at its dying close
The soul seemed melting in the trembling breast;
The eye in dews of pity flowed away,
And every heart, by sorrow's load opprest,
To infant softness sunk, as breathed thy mournful lay."

—James Percival

On October 7, 1914, Frederic Gerhard left his home at 923 West Market Street shortly after seven o'clock in the evening. His last words leaving the house were jocular; in fact, his distraught wife thought that he had been in high spirits during their dinner. She never imagined that he would be dead three hours later. While seated at the downtown Sphinx Club, Fred Gerhard talked and joked with fellow members, when his head dropped suddenly toward the table. He gasped for breath, complaining of nausea and severe pains in his head. He was taken to a private room and made comfortable by his companions. Reverend Reiter, the pastor of Trinity Reformed Church, the pastor who presided over the Simon services in 1909, was at the Sphinx Club and calmly gave some words of encouragement to his stricken friend before summoning Mrs. Gerhard. He then prayed over his friend.

Believing it to be a bad case of indigestion, Professor Gerhard managed to get up and place himself in a reclining chair. "All I need is some rest, boy. I must of scared everyone." He then closed his eyes and sat serenely, but by 9:30 the musician cannot be aroused and an ambulance was summoned. Sadly, the patient was taken, not to the hospital, but back to his home and carried into his house. At 10:15 P.M. he breathed his last breath. Besides his bed stood not only his wife and two children, but also several of his dear friends. Reverend Reiter announced to the people that gathered in the living room that the famed musician had died peacefully. "Coal region hospitality" is a short phrase that came to life that night and resonated as hundreds of people stopped by the house to give comfort to the troubled family. It certainly had not been a bad case of indigestion as everyone suspected at first. No, an era of musical greatness was now at an end in Pottsville, Pottsville, brought about by cardiac arrest.

"Professor Gerhard is dead."

His funeral was one of the largest in Pottsville's history with the overwhelming crowd spilling from the English Lutheran Church onto Garfield Square, listening to the inspiring words of Reverend Reiter, listening and weeping to the young blind girl named Mabel Toole who sang a woeful soprano rendition of hymn for divide guidance. "Lead, kindly Light, amid the encircling gloom, Lead thou me on! The night is dark, and I am far from home, Lead thou me on!" Not a dry eye in the church was seen, as the young soloist was led back to her church pew.

Thanatos was very pleased that night.

Those outside the church watched the large procession of musicians as the cortège circled Garfield Square. This was the Square that the beloved Professor presided at during the great centennial celebration in 1906. Many followed the carriage carrying his casket up Market Street as the procession slowly headed towards the final resting place at Presbyterian cemetery. At the gravesite twenty musicians play a Gerhard arrangement of "Taps," as the casket is gently lowered into the ground. After the last note is played, the only sound heard was the woeful sound of the shovels scooping up dirt to cover the remains of dear Professor Gerhard.

Some say fate, while others believe it to be just a coincidence that Gerhard died shortly before the destruction of the Academy of Music. How odd that his beloved music hall would burn to the ground on December 17, 1914, in the most destructive fire in Pottsville's history, with flames running across the Greek images that adorned the theatre.

In the end, the Academy of Music was totally destroyed. The fire takes, not only the prized theatre, but also almost the entire block of South Centre Street—including Miehle's Department Store. Some observers say that the Fred Gerhard would have died of a broken heart if he were alive that fiery December night. The Academy of Music is no more; its empty site will always remain as a hole in the heart of Pottsville.

Melpomene and Thanatos' work was now done. They would leave for Europe, as Archduke Ferdinand had been assassinated in Sarajevo, thereby igniting World War I. The two Muses would be kept very busy over the next several years, certain to meet up with some young Pottsville boys in due course.

Only in a matter of time.

CHAPTER 21

▼

YEARS AFTER THE CENTENNIAL

So, your story is being written for Pottsville's upcoming 150th anniversary. Hell, I will be 72 years old then. Maybe I will grow a beard and become a brother of the brush or whatever. I'm almost finished my story. I hope you enjoyed it. I hope it can be used in telling the history of my town. As for the anniversary, all anniversaries now get me depressed, but I certainly will raise my glass high and toast Pottsville and remember all of those wonderful people. I will even say a prayer for the souls of the Simon family.

Jack Quinn, in 1914, played ball for the Boston Braves in the National League. He continued pitching for 23 years, winning 247 games in three different major leagues for eight teams. He pitched against Hall of Fame shortstops George Davis and Arky Vaughan, and became a teammate with Hall of Fame hurlers Chief Bender and Lefty Grove. In 1929, Quinn started the fourth game of the World Series for Connie Mack's A's at the mature age of 46, and the next season he again pitched in the Series. During the regular season in 1930, he became the oldest man to hit a home run in the major leagues. The right-hander pitched his final game for Cincinnati in 1933 at the age of 50, posting a respectable 4.02 ERA in 15 innings of relief works.

After his retirement, Jack retired in Pottsville where he was still known to many as Jack Picus. He resided in the local downtown Eagle Hotel, passing away in 1946. Connie Mack sent a personal note of condolence to his family but was unable to attend the services held under the supervision of funeral director and mayor, Claude A. Lord, who was just a young lad in the centennial year. Jack Picus Quinn is now at rest with many other former notables in the community's beautiful park-like cemetery.

Entering through the massive stone arches, the Charles Baber Cemetery invites the living with its serene, winding paths, canopy of trees, and pristine pond. It is the jewel of the city, with the solemn Resurrection Chapel as its center. It cannot be described as a mournful place. On the contrary, the public was invited in to ice skate, listen to the occasional concerts given by the Third Brigade Band, and participate in pigeon shoot competitions. Picnics generally followed the latter event, and it was not uncommon to see entire families remain for a day's worth of entertainment within the stone cemetery walls.

Yes, it is at this Victorian community burial field that Jack Picus Quinn was reunited with Cincinnati Reds first baseman, Jake Daubert, buried not too far away.

As for Charlemagne Tower, Jr., after retiring from international service, he continued to manage his family fortune. He received many honors during his lifetime, including the French Legion of Honor, a prestigious honor conferred upon men and women, whether a French citizen or not, for outstanding achievements in military or civil life. Another honor was the Russian Order of St. Alexander Nevsky, an award originated by Peter the Great, and bestowed on notable civilians as well as military heroes. Tower death occurs on February 24, 1923 in Philadelphia.

The millionaire club man, J. Barlow Cullum, whose mansion was devastated by the fire of 1907, did rebuild, and he continued to live there on Howard Avenue in winter months, while spending the other months in Europe. He finally sold the premises in 1918 after he became interested in the raising of registered Guernsey cattle. To pursue this new passion, the Cullums purchased a large farm in Bern Township, Berks County, called "Riverside Farms." This large home is the present clubhouse of the Berkshire County Club. Mr. Cullum died in 1933 after a lengthy illness. His remains were buried in the Milliken family plot in Baber Cemetery. His wife, Anne, would be buried next to her husband and her parents, after her death in 1950. She died while vacationing in Miami Beach.

George F. Baer remained at the head of the Reading Company until his death in Philadelphia on April 26, 1914, just shy of age 72, achieving the distinction of being one of the oldest chief railroad executives in the nation. He left behind a fortune estimated at $15 million. On the day of his funeral the Pottsville headquarters closed, and a large local delegation attended the simple services. The idea to idle all of the railroads for a short period of time in his honor had been abandoned as impractical. Mr. Baer would have wanted the railroads to run uninterrupted in any event.

1917 united two life-long friends for all eternity. Charles Napoleon Brumm, the cranky seventy-nine year old judge passed away in January. Jack Crawford, the man who humbly introduced himself to crowds as a boy soldier, rustic poet, Indian scout, and bad actor when he campaigned for his dear friend Charlie Brumm in 1906, the centennial year, joined Brumm in the hereafter the following month. He died quietly from pneumonia at his Long Island, New York home. Crawford used the title "bad actor" in reference to his 1915 motion picture debut in "Battle Cry of Peace." Coincidentally, Buffalo Bill Cody, another good friend of Crawford, as well as his role model, who often visited Pottsville, died one week before Charles Brumm.

Needless to say Buffalo Bill had the most grandiose funeral of the three.

Notwithstanding the election of a mayor in 1913, the guerrilla warfare of the opponents of the charter continued through 1914 with the filing of various legal challenges in the courts. The determined opponents hoped that the charter would be declared unconstitutional. On July 1st of that year, the Pennsylvania Supreme Court unanimously ruled, "the entire proceedings under which the borough of Pottsville became a city of the third class must be deemed regular and valid."

Those who had supported the charter over the years shouted, "The long struggle against the vested interests was over!"

After the city council hired a new police chief, Hiram Davies successfully ran for a council seat in 1916. I guess he was thinking, "If you can't beat them, join them." It worked for him, as he remained a power to be reckoned with, especially in the polling places of his Sixth Ward. After leaving his short stint on council, Davies was hired as a county deputy sheriff before becoming a local alderman. Upon his final retirement he built an attractive home in Schuylkill Haven, staying only one year, as he missed his hometown of Pottsville dearly. He purchased a house on Mahantongo Street, Pottsville's own "rue des rêves," but before his death in 1935 he moved, for the last time, to George Street, the same street where George Simon years before had committed his terrible crime. Claude A. Lord, once again, had the honors of hosting a dignified funeral service for the last police chief of Pottsville's burgess system.

Martha Ridgway Bannan, the grand matriarch of Pottsville, passed on at the age of 92 in 1933. She had lived through the ages of the stagecoach, canal boat, locomotive, automobile and airplane, always contented to be in tune with the times. She was a connection with Pottsville's past, and irreplaceable. With her death a glorious chapter of the city's history was completed. While most women of her era were raised to be quiet housewives, having no opinions on political or social issues, Miss Bannan took another path.

Dr. John George Striegel, who had not been at the hangings as he was still in medical school, would not be remembered for his medical practice, but would become a legend in the community for his promotion of football. Not unlike many thriving communities, Pottsville fielded a football team prior to World War I, but it would not be until after the Great War that Pottsville got really serious about football. In fact, the whole eastern Pennsylvania-New Jersey area underwent a pro football explosion in the early 1920's, with particularly strong teams in Philadelphia and Atlantic City. The quality of football was arguably on a par with the Midwest-centered NFL. Pottsville's team held its own against the best of them. In 1925 Striegel's team, The Maroons, would forever be shrouded in controversy involving the 1925 NFL Championship. The Maroons and the team's "stolen championship" would immortalize Striegel as part of Pottsville's history.

And what of Cornelius Foley, the outspoken barber? He also lived on to the early 1930s. His barbershop continued to be a busy male retreat. Amid the cigar fumes and bay rum, city men congregated and browsed through the spicy pages of the Police Gazette, waiting for an inexpensive shave and haircut while listening to Foley's interpretation of current events. Con Foley's life was one of continuous excitement and activity, unquestionably placing a strain on his sixty-year-old heart. Realizing for months that his condition was terminal and his days were numbered, he used the telephone next to his bed to espouse his views on every issue brought to his attention to friends and sympathizers who called. He died at his house, coincidentally located at the corner of East Norwegian and North George Street; a few blocks from the old Simon house.

Joel Boone was destined for an illustrious career. The young man joined the navy and would later be awarded the Congressional Medal of Honor for gallantry in France during World War I. After the armistice, he was chosen as one of the honorary pallbearers at the internment of the Unknown Soldier. He eventually was appointed an Admiral and served as the personal physician for presidents Harding, Coolidge and Hoover. During the Hoover administration, Boone also had professional contact with such celebrity patients as Marie Curie, Thomas

Alva Edison, and Henry Ford. Yes, Joel Boone, a schoolmate of George Simon, who sang with George in the glee club, had a glorious career.

And what of the old Simon house? The residence no longer exists, having been demolished in some unknown year. Gone, too, are all of the secrets the house held.

As for public hangings in Pottsville, they ceased after the death of Joseph Chistock on March 30, 1911. That spectacle attracted the usual crowd of approximately 1,000. Women that attempted to get into the prison yard were politely turned away. The wretched Chistock, who fatally shot a woman during a robbery, boasted to reporters that if he had the opportunity he would have killed more people. However, in the final moments of his pathetic life, he thanked his guards for their kindness before asking Almighty God for forgiveness. After the lever was pulled and the prisoner's lifeless corpse swayed to and fro, the warden admonished the crowd not to attempt take any part of the rope for a souvenir.

Tisiphone, Megaera and Alecto, known collectively as the Furies, would have to go elsewhere.

After that execution, the state of Pennsylvania took responsibility for carrying out death sentences. Pottsville had seen its last one as in 1916, Mike Louissa, given a death sentence in the Pottsville Courthouse, was put to death at Rockview Penitentiary. He was strapped onto "Old Smokey," the state's first electric chair. The crowds from Schuylkill County could not watch.

As for the city, founded by entrepreneur John Pott in 1806, it continued to take on the cosmopolitan air of a big city, at least for a while. During the 1930s and 1940s its sidewalks filled with people going to the numerous stores. Its downtown became one of the liveliest, bustling business districts in the state. For a city of less than 25,000 the number of stores boggled one's mind. Within a short walking distance there were several furriers, department stores, jewelry stores and many, many specialty shops. Alas, Nothing lasts forever. Anthracite coal production peaked in 1917, bringing with it high employment. Coal was needed to fight the Great War. After the war ended, anthracite was being replaced as the major fuel supply of the nation. World War II gave another shot in the arm to the anthracite region, but the writing is on the wall that oil and gas are replacing coal's importance as the nation's fuel. In 1947 developers started to construct Levittown in Bucks County. The desire for the middle class to settle outside of cities will intensify. Pottsville will be no exception. As for shopping, in Enida, Minnesota the first fully enclosed shopping mall is scheduled to open in 1956, the year of Pottsville's 150th birthday. The Shopping Mall concept, with its free parking, will spread like wildfire and signal an end to the reign of city shopping. In addition employment opportunities are heading west. Pennsylvania had long been the second most populous state, behind New York, but in 1950 it fell to third due to the growth of California.

Pottsville will certainly have its hands full in the next fifty years, and hopefully William Shakespeare will be proven correct on his quote that "The wheel of life would come full circle."

Acknowledgments and Comments

The primary sources utilized were the Pottsville Republican and Miners Journal newspapers, both published in Pottsville and available on microfilm at the Historical Society of Schuylkill County. Other sources include: The Anthracite Aristocracy: leadership and social change in the hard coal regions of northeastern Pennsylvania, 1800–1930, by Edward J. Davies II (Northern Illinois University Press, 1985), History of Schuylkill County (J.H. Beers & Company 1916), Victorian America: Transformations in Everyday Life 1876–1915, by Thomas J.Schlereth (HarperPerennial 1992), The J.H. Zerbey History, Pottsville and Schuylkill County, Penna, Pottsville High School Yearbooks 1906, 1907, 1908, 1909, WPSX, Dictionary of American Biography. New York: C. Scribner, 1928–96; "By The Light Of The Silvery Moon" by Gus Edwards and Edward Madden; "Take Me Out to the Ball Game," words by Jack Norworth (1908), and editing assistance by Mark Major.

The book is intended to be a glimpse into one Pennsylvania town during a short critical period of ten years (1906–1916).

Obviously, certain dialogue, when not based on newspaper quotes, was created with the best intent of conveying what the characters may have reasonably said. This was done selectively, hoping to gain a better perspective of the characters and the time period. Such a goal obviously requires some minor modification of the events. For instance, while the two financial giants, Charlemagne Tower, Jr. and George Baer, did take a carriage ride through the downtown, the conversation was created to give the reader a sense of what the downtown was like at that point in time. There were no transcripts of what the two gentlemen actually talked about. Likewise the interrogation of George Simon, Sr. was re-created through the newspaper quotes with the addition of some basic police interrogation questions. The police raid on the West Norwegian Street home did occur and was the subject of major newspaper accountings. However, certain minor additions, such as the Victrola playing in the parlor, were done for the sole purpose of anchoring the setting in its proper time frame—the birth of the recorded music age and the automobile age. The only purely fictional parts of the book were the card game at the Pottsville Club that occurs after the homicide and, of course, the Greek Mythological allegories.

978-0-595-36559-3
0-595-36559-0

Made in the USA
Lexington, KY
05 October 2010